GASLAMPS, GUNSMOKE,
AND GOTHIKA

———•———

THE
HONEYSUCKLE
HORROR

W.M. SOUTHERLAND

Special Thanks

I'd like to thank a couple of very special people without whom this book--and likely any future books of mine--would not exist, starting with my mother. Now this is a woman with whom I have *very* often disagreed with and fully expect to continue doing so, however she is also among the only people in my life I'd trust with almost anything. She's always striven to ride the line between supporting me unconditionally and pushing me to stand on my own two feet. Yes there have been times that I would have much preferred her to do the former, I'll always respect her commitment to the latter. Thanks, mom.

Secondly, I would like to thank my partner. She has been flexible, supportive, understanding, and encouraging in all the most perfect ways possible. I love her and I couldn't have done this (let alone come out sane at the end) without her love and commitment. Thank you so much, you're my favorite.

Thirdly, I'd like to extend my gratitude to the incredible and inexorable online content creators whose hard work and due diligence gave me the opportunity and tools I needed to learn, practice, and maybe someday master this craft free of charge. I cannot possibly overstate just how amazing it was to be able to gain so much knowledge, so much experience, and so much feedback (however indirect) without having to start an often uncompensated career with mountains of debt. I'll list a few of their names and YouTube channels below, but this is in no way an exhaustive list. To all of you, thank you!

- Timothy Hickson of *Hello Future Me,* author of *On Writing and Worldbuilding: Volume I* and *II*
- Linsay Ellis of *Lindsay Ellis* and PBS's *Storied,* author of *Axiom's End*
- Melina Pendulum of *Melina Pendulum* and PBS's *Storied*

- "Red" and "Blue" of *Overly Sarcastic Productions*
- John and Hank Green of (most notably) *Crash Course*. Both are incredible novelists. Examples of their works include *The Fault in Our Stars* by John Green and *An Absolutely Remarkable Thing* by Hank Green.
- Many many others whose long work and commitment to sharing their knowledge with others. Thank you all!

Finally, I'd like to thank the team at Coalescence Publishing. These people are committed to creating a positive and inclusive experience for creatives to hone their craft and have the opportunity to receive all the benefits of a supportive publishing studio without the crushing pressure that being under a larger house often brings. They gave me an opportunity I wouldn't have found elsewhere and they gave me the support of a network of peers that creatives often need. They gave me push, they gave me drive, they gave me an environment where I could share my ideas without being judged, and for all of that, thanks y'all.

1.

The townsfolk of Verdendale bustled as the morning light peeled over the Wichitook Caldera into the Alpwood. It was springtime on the frontier and around that time of year, the forest around Verdendale was a sight to see. Wildflowers colonized the woodland floor and blossoming vines crawled their way up the tree trunks, all decorating the landscape with vibrant colors that interrupted the emerald hue of the river valley.

In addition to this, the sounds of the region's fauna waking in the morning were much like a symphonic overture. The birdsong was a melody given percussion from time to time by the sounds of a woodpecker boring into the home of its prey. All harmonized by uncountable species of insects, mammals, and noisy amphibians.

Verdendale itself was not a small city. It was founded along the Kuedino River which stretched from the Shevic Mountains in the West into the coast of the Uga-dariac Sea. There were a dozen hotels, half that number of taphouses, a handful of other craftsmen most of whom existed to fulfill the needs of the town's true industry: wine. The fields between the village and forests were almost entirely vineyards, only narrowly interrupted by roads. Verdendale produced some of the best wine of the frontier, the most famous of which was Honeysuckle Mead.

A brief history of the town might mention when Verdendale was founded by its first baron alongside a group of settlers when they discovered a rampant breed of enormous honeysuckle weeds the blossoms of which were so large that a single one could yield a small vial's worth of potent nectar. When the settlers began growing wine, they naturally experimented with the substance until they'd concocted a potable vintage. The product grew their settlement from a small stop up-river into one of the most successful baronies of the northern expanse.

So vital was the vintage that the first barons of Verdendale dubbed the Spring Equinox to be a day of celebration when the oldest vintage was to be brought to the markets. The celebration was named the Honeysuckle Festival and over the last two decades, the Baron always returned to their Verdendale Estate to host the festival on the eve of the celebration. Today was that day, and how excited the people were for its coming.

Today, times were grim, even in the serene forests and fields of the Alpwood. All about the town, one could hear men cursing the local bands of natives, spitting out such curses as, "dark-skinned devils." Stories abounded of 'wild men' with bows and sorcery attacking patrols and disrupting caravans. Tales were spun of entire fields being set aflame moments after strange native tongues echoed through the night.

The next breath was typically spent in praise of Lord Brigmond, the new Prime Minister of the United Baronies of Alasthia, the name for the imperial province which dominated the frontier. Gossip spoke of a short, broad man with a strong voice that carried over crowds of thousands. The man was an activist of piety, accredited with inviting the Fraternal Church of St. Alasthine and their "Paladin Legions" to assist the provincial government in protecting society from the added threat of the "native insurgents and foreign wizardry."

This new police force had curbed many of the fears of the common law-abiding imperial citizen, yet a palpable shift in the atmosphere could be felt in every settlement west of the capital of Alatine. As engineers developed technologies that brought down the craftsman and elevated the industrialist, the popular zeitgeist found itself in sorcery and immorality. So far, only the big cities of the east coast had been affected by this, yet the news from these places spoke mixed messages to the rural folk of Verdendale.

Some migrants spoke of prosperity, opportunity, and living like kings. Others told a different tale, speaking of oppression, slavery in workhouses where hot metal machinery boiled the skin and poisoned the air with clouds of stinking smog. All of these tales perplexed the people of Verdendale, or most of the people anyway.

On the riverfront down the hill from the Baron's estate dwelled one of the town's few remaining blacksmiths. Donard by name, he was a dwarf and this dwarf was little concerned with the problems of industrialism. Each day he simply woke from sleep and prepared himself for the day's work. He paid scarce attention to zeitgeists, much preferring to keep to himself and his craft, which mainly focused on repairs and supplies for the riverboats transporting people and goods up and down the Kuedino. This morning, he got up and went to his hearth to boil water for his morning tea--as was his usual routine--before a knock startled him from his half-woken malaise.

Grumbling, Donard went to his door and opened it to see a poncily dressed man with a pencil thin mustache standing on his doorstep. "We're closed today." Donard put simply and went to close the door.

Bumbling forward in an attempt to keep the door ajar, the man spoke with a high pitched voice that made the smith's headache. "Oh, no, good sir. I'm not here for metalwork. I'm here on behalf of…"

"I don't care. Go away." and that was that. The door was swung shut, and Infryd quite hoped it hit the gangly man in his aquiline nose to make sure the message was well understood. He poured his tea and sat on his back porch facing the mountains of the aforementioned caldera, smoked tobacco from a corn-cob pipe.

He'd never actually been inside the caldera but the sun looked beautiful rising above the peaks and he always wondered what the world within the ring of high cliffs looked like. He'd heard of thick forests, massive geysers, and fields of hot springs. Of course, none of it sounded more magnificent than Mount Wichitooka itself. A titanic lone peak in the center of this "new world," nothing less than godlike in proportion to even one not living with dwarfism.

Here on his porch, Donard chewed on his pipe and wondered what that throne of the gods looked like, but as usual he shook away his musings, finished his tea, and knocked the burnt tobacco out onto his sleeve before pulling his suspenders over his shoulders and turning in for a day at the forge. This was where Donard spent the rest of his day, beard tucked into his apron with his hands and face covered in soot. He forged nails, fitted hammers to handles, and even toiled over a couple of decorative sabers contracted by riverboat captains. He did not enjoy this work in the slightest, but it was a good cover at least.

2.

Up the hill from Donard's forge, an exquisite form rose from its bed on the third floor of the Baron's Estate. This particular form was of a youth born to the rich class of medicinal scientists in a distant arid province named Khuttania far in the southeastern side of the empire. The form belonged to a woman named Ifra Al-Jintra, and for all her pedigree, she'd found herself under the patronage of a lowly frontier baron.

Some time ago, the headmaster of her school had received a request from Verdendale for a doctor to serve at his estate after the unfortunate defection of his previous employee who'd joined a rebellion led by some penniless western earl. In response, the headmaster chose his model student to travel to Verdendale and serve this Baron. The journey from Khuttania was long, but Ifra was eager to begin researching the medical advances made in the Baronies. All the journey long she'd daydreamed of presenting a thesis on the subject to her peers when she returned.

She was sorely disappointed to find the physician's laboratory empty. Her predecessor had made off with nearly every tool and piece of literature, leaving not a single herb or alembic. Thus, Ifra's first day in a new land had been spent making a list of supplies for the majordomo to send for. That was two days ago, and only a nominal number of the requested packages had arrived.

This morning was the morning of a grand feast at the estate, a fact that only served to add to Ifra's anxiety. Being in the estate, the doctor's main focus would be on the Baron and his family when they arrived, seconded by the noble guests in attendance. As she understood it, honor duels with firearms were something of a regularity in these circles, rendering the need for her services great and the lack of supplies quite damning.

However, the rest of the estate's staff were in good spirits about the whole ordeal causing Ifra to wonder if perhaps she was just misunderstanding the severity of frontier incredulity. This morning, Ifra woke to a knock on the door of her third-floor room. "Who is it?" She asked, rising from the bed.

"It's the laundry maid, miss. I've been tasked to bring you your festive attire for the evening."

"Very well, if you could just leave it by the door…"

"Oh, I shan't be doing that, miss. I'll not be soilin' it with dust or wrinkles. It's hand-woven, miss."

"Ah, well, just a moment then." Ifra went to the door and cracked it. "If you could, just hand them to me, I can manage."

"Oh, no, I shan't be doin' that miss! I'll be helpin' you put it on. We must avoid it gettin' tears or otherwise."

The woman is rather insistent for a servant, Ifra thought. Annoyed, she opened the door and bid the old maid come in. The woman, careful not to wrinkle the silken garments, squeezed through the cracks and set the outfit flat on the bed, every motion done with absolute intent.

When she turned and looked at Ifra, she gasped a little and put a hand to her mouth as if trying to cover her blushing cheeks. "My heavens, if you don't mind me sayin' miss, you are truly radiant. Skin like milk and coffee!"

Ifra winced a little, feigning gratitude at what was at least meant to be a compliment, and cleared her throat. "I should really be getting to my work, though. Could you just leave the garments on the dresser over there?"

"Not a chance, miss. We haven't had the chance to dust that dresser yet. We can'ny risk soilin' it."

"Alright," Ifra pressed her lips together in obvious frustration that the old maid seemed to either ignore or miss entirely, "I suppose I'll put it on now, then."

"Indeed you will, miss." With that the maid began meticulously unfolding the garment. "What's your name, miss? If you don't mind me askin'."

"It's 'doctor' actually, and my name is Ifra bint Sabadi al-Jintra."

"Oh! That's a long name miss, do you go by anything different?"

"Madam, as I said, it's not 'miss' but 'doctor' and no, I don't go by anything different. Why would I?"

"Oh, my apologies miss, I meant no offense. It's just that perhaps it might make things easier on those who don't speak your language, is all."

"We speak Darian in my country, madam. Our names stem from languages spoken before the empire came."

"Oh? Why don't you use Darian names, then? They're a lot shorter at least."

Ifra contained herself, as a short tingle of anger sent chills over her body. "Are you almost done, madam?"

"I'm just tyin' the last thread miss, no need to rush."

"Alright!" Ifra smacked away the old woman's hands. "I think I can handle one thread madam, please allow me to see you out."

"My dear miss, I meant no offense…"

Ifra pushed the old woman out of the room and before shutting the door, stated in no uncertain terms, "It's 'doctor,' woman. Not 'miss.' I am a physician, I spent my life studying every aspect of these mortal shells we call 'bodies' and I refuse to have my station denied to me, now be on your way."

After shutting the door, she heard the old woman proclaim, "Well you're not going to make that many friends here being rude like that miss." Ifra's eyes twitched a little at that, then she took a moment to breathe as the servant's steps sounded more and more faint. Ifra looked down at the clothes she'd been made to wear. Though it seemed the

Baron had ordered them tailored for her, Ifra thought the clothes looked both ugly and uncomfortable.

Finally, Ifra left her room and descended the servant's stairwell to the second floor, and traveled through the corridors to the laboratory. The windows were open, allowing the sun to irradiate the room with a golden morning glow reminding Ifra of her room in the tower where the medical scholars of the Mujama Al-Mughraba were housed. There, high above the city streets below, the sun seemed almost at eye level with her, as if they could greet each other like good friends every morning and bid farewell in the evening.

Here, so low to the ground, the sun was already high in the sky, reinforcing in the lonely Ifra's feeling of homesickness that only a foreigner in a foreign land can know, and none else can describe. This was made all the worse by the distinct lack of supplies in this small lab that persisted even after three days of requests to the Majordomo.

She thought that she might have to venture into the woods to procure what herbal ingredients she could find there, but decided that it might not be proper by these people's standards to sally out and get filthy while formally dressed. Any solution to the emptiness of her shelves seemed to carry some weighty form of indiscretion or invalidity, so the dismayed Ifra resigned herself to the predicament, struggling to adopt the same optimism about the coming festivities as her hosts.

Outside her laboratory, the majordomo was walking toward the foyer. He was an old man with a hooked nose and small beady eyes, nothing remaining of his hair except a thick white wreath around his crown. He stepped and stood just outside the laboratory door. His dress was regal and themed to greens and golds not unlike that which had been given to Ifra herself. "Goodmorning, doctor. I hope the attire is to your liking." Ifra felt relieved to at least hear someone recognize her position.

Ifra cleared her throat and said, "It is fine, thank you."

The majordomo nodded his head in agreement, looking up and down Ifra's body. "Yes, it does seem to fit you well."

"It does, however it *is* a fair Spring day. I must ask, are such long sleeves necessary?"

"Do you take issue with sleeves, doctor?"

"It just seems a little out of season, wouldn't you say?"

"The nobility of the Baronies tend to prefer a bit of prudence when it comes to dress attire. I'm sure you understand."

"Of course."

With that, the majordomo gestured down the corridor, "Now if you'll please follow me, I'd like to give you a proper tour of the estate and the areas that will be populated during tonight's festivities."

Ifra nodded and they began to weave their way through the myriad halls of the palace. The doctor was happy to be with the majordomo as she was sure she'd have gotten lost without a guide, at least the first time through.

"Why are all the staff adorned with such colors?" Ifra asked after noticing a number of other servants guised in green and gold.

"It's a tradition of the Honeysuckle Festival to wear colors reminiscent of the season. The lord High Baron has dubbed that all inside the estate be adorned in green and gold this year."

"And where is the High Baron? I've yet to see him in my time here."

"My lord has been away from the estate most of the year. His duties drew him to the parliamentary court in St. Alasthine to the east. He'll be back for the festival though."

"Such a long time to be gone. What business has been keeping him in the provincial capitol so?"

"Alasthia isn't a province, it's an independent state, regardless of the empire's ability to make amendments to our constitution. However, some seem incapable of accepting even the relatively little oversight our dominion does receive from the empress. Rebellion is spreading across the south and the Baron has been working the courts for cooperative ties in the event of a declaration of war upon the secessionists."

"I'll admit, I find all this a little confusing." Ifra stated. "The empire's presence is so lax here compared to their influence in my home province."

"Well, we are an ocean apart. Much further than your country is from the imperial heartlands. The Dominionary Parliament has kept close ties with the empress, and that has given us a measure of support and autonomy most other provinces don't have."

"And yet?" Ifra stopped and eyed the old man quizzically.

"And yet, it seems to have caused some among the Barons to feel apprehensive at even the slightest level of oversight."

"And that's cause for war?"

"If they start shooting, then yes." With that they continued winding down the corridors.

The hallways opened to the great foyer, which seemed to Ifra as more of a ballroom for its size. Three massive crystal chandeliers hung from a vaulted ceiling painted to depict an epic battle of red-cloaked heroes against a horde of monstrous foes. Three great pillars on either side of the room rose to join the war, from each of their tops protruding four great gargoyles, to which some of the heroes of the mural rushed for battle.

Down the stairs from the banister where the doctor and the majordomo stood, the house servants scurried around cleaning and putting the finishing touches on the green and gold decorations. Bouquets of flowers colored every surface with an array of violets, fuchsias, carmines, and indigos. It was the most colorful display Ifra had ever seen.

Just then, two men entered the foyer from the dining room of the North Wing. One was dressed quite nicely and the other was, while still wearing green and gold, obviously not of the same echelon. "Be sure that the peasants outside only get a quarter of a glass of mead, diluted. We shan't be wasting the High Baron's produce on those who haven't paid for it." The finely dressed one said to the other.

"Shall we supply them with cider beyond that then, mister chamberlain sir?" Asked the other.

"Yes, all the mead and wine will be served to the High Baron's noble guests here inside the palace. Conservatively on the mead, of course. We've already set the allotment for the evening to ensure we still have enough to export down the Kuedino. As for wine, our profits will be high enough to allow the lord's guests their fill."

"As you say, mister chamberlain sir." The other hurried off, presumably to give the instructions to the rest of the staff.

"Goodmorning, Mister Royce." the Majordomo said as they descended the banister stairs.

"Goodmorning to you, Mister Kariakis." the chamberlain replied.

"Doctor al-Jintra, may I introduce you to the Baron's chamberlain, cabinet member Kirkland Royce. Chamberlain, this is Doctor Ifra bint Sabadi al-Jintra, Mr. Delerict's replacement."

"Charmed, I'm sure," the Chamberlain responded. Ifra wondered if the chamberlain was afflicted with some sort of cold. His voice was heavily nasal and his nose was turned up slightly. His two front teeth were a bit larger than the rest, giving him the most kindred appearance to a rat

14

that Ifra had yet seen amongst humans. "It would seem my suspicions were right then and we've gone from hiring filthy wizards to barbarian sorceresses."

"Sir Chamberlain, would you cast an insult on our lord's decision?" The Majordomo asked indignantly.

"Oh, I highly doubt it was his decision, Mister Kariakis. More than likely it was made by one of his councilors in the capital, perhaps in an effort to facilitate relations with this woman's people." The Chamberlain scoffed heavily. "The last doctor was practicing witchcraft and ran off to join a band of upstarts in the south, but at least he knew it was witchcraft. The peoples of Movania practice blasphemy and call it 'science,' deluded as they are."

The Majordomo was about to raise a word in protest, but Ifra spoke first. "Mister Royce, I assure you that you won't see me dancing around a fire or whispering incantations to wounds. There is a method to science that allows us to answer more questions than the compounding mysteries of the supernatural. My devices are entirely founded on this method, on critical analysis and peer review. I am no more a sorceress than you are a butler."

"That remains to be seen, Miss al-Jintra." the chamberlain said in spite of Ifra's intellectual response. "More likely, your devices are magical machines designed to rob us of every last coin we own. Now, unless you're going to further regale me with falsehoods, I have our lord's business to attend to. The High Baron requires more profits this year. These nativist brigands in the hills have disturbed our caravans such that we must prioritize our river trade goods. That includes Honeysuckle Mead." With that, the Chamberlain sauntered away.

"It's *Doctor* al-Jintra, Mister Royce." Ifra called as he walked away.

"Charming fellow, him." the Majordomo said once the chamberlain was out of earshot. "He has a quick wit when it comes to industry but has always been quite dim with regards to manners. I hope you'll forgive him for his failings."

"It's quite alright, Mister Kariakis. I suspect his opinions are shared by most." Ifra replied.

The Majordomo cleared his throat and started walking again, this time toward the entrance of the estate. "At any rate, I must be about my business, as I am sure it is true for you as well. Perhaps you'll join our tour of the palace grounds when the High Baron's noble guests arrive later this afternoon."

"I look forward to it." Ifra gave a curt bow and the Majordomo returned it and left him standing in the middle of the massive chamber.

3.

Down the hill from the palace, a host of large tents interspersed with stalls and stages decorated an open field just outside the borders of the town. Music filled the area, alongside the smell of sweets and oily foods. It was all quite outlandish to the people of Verdendale, and especially to the emissary of the estate sent down the hill with a message for the proprietor of this establishment, or event, or whatever the right word is for a traveling circus.

The proprietor's name was Bimblewald, Octavius Bimblewald, and he'd been bringing his Cirque du Freak to the Honeysuckle Festival since he founded it nearly a decade ago. It never failed to please the sleepy crowds of Verdendale with its bizarre displays of foreign talents and skills, not to mention the general abnormality of the carnival's employees. Many were disfigured or deformed, and even those that weren't physically unseemly were behaving unseemly. Though there appeared to be a large overlap between the two.

Jesters dressed in bright clothing adorned with bells and painted their faces with expressions of utmost lethargy or otherwise pleasure. They pantomimed invisible obstacles and filled little balloons, folding them into shapes of animals or other objects. Magicians, though certainly not practitioners of true wizardry, baffled the people with sleight-of-hand and suggestion, manipulating the crowds with the greatest of ease.

Years ago when the Cirque was first founded, the latter of these performances drew suspicion from the authorities. After a brief investigation, however, the people were assured that none of the Cirque's magicians were enchanting the people in any arcane sense, and thus the people engaged with the entertainment free of guilt or fear. A fact that made Mister Bimblewald quite relieved, what with the pitchforks remaining dull and the torches unlit.

Fools (as opposed to the jesters) danced about in dunce caps without a care in the world, causing children to dance and giggle madly along with them, carrying their little rubber toys and sporting foolish hats of their own. Once said children were done running amok, they might have visited one of the stalls pilfering greasy foods cooked with flour and boiling oil.

Finally, later in the afternoon, performances of jugglers, acrobats, tight-rope walkers, horsemen, animal tamers, and fire-breathers would tantalize the senses of each and every visitor before releasing them to ascend the hill and galavant the night away on the High Baron's liquor while the children were encouraged to stay with the troop and listen to the reading of stories. It was truly a triumph of mirth, just as Mr. Bimblewald wished.

It was about midday now, and the emissary trudged through the swathes of peasants, his green and gold brocade suit causing him to sweat in the noonday sun. This was, of course, not at all abated by the collective heat of a township's worth of activity. Yet, the man trudged on, careful not to step in areas that seemed particularly muddied, until he reached a little tent on the far edge of the circus.

Outside, a giant of a man sat on a "stool," if it could be called such a thing given its size. It certainly seemed like a stool to this creature. The emissary approached, and the giant thing opened its eyes, making the gentleman notice for the first time that the creature had the head of an average human, but a body *largely* out of proportion. His face seemed to be disfigured as well, one eye bulging out even further than its elongated forehead.

The thing attempted to stand but didn't seem able to without great effort. It, or he, or she (the emissary wasn't quite able to ascertain how best to refer to the creature before him in his mind) made some stuttering noises and blubbered about the emissary's fine clothing before

18

opening the canvas door and gesturing the man inside. The interior of the tent seemed washed with a red hue as the sunlight broke through the painted canvas, and the emissary's light sweat broke into heavy perspiration as he entered.

Before him, a desk sat half sunken in the soft dirt. Behind the desk, a man he could only presume was Octavius Bimblewald sat with a top hat covering his eyes and his feet atop the aforementioned piece of furniture. The carnie let out a light snore, begging the emissary to clear his throat loudly.

Not much was needed to wake the middle-aged fellow and he snapped his head up, lifting the top hat to sit loosely on his crown. "Well hello there, my good man. What brings you to my tent, this fine day? Hopefully, it's not to inquire about a refund, because I'm afraid we don't offer those."

The emissary wasn't expecting a well-spoken man in Bimblewald. Taken aback slightly, he held out a letter sealed with the High Baron's insignia. "Good sir Bimblewald, the Baron, his lordship Leonard Balteshezzar II would like to express his most sincere thanks for the business that your circus brings to the town and the barony by presenting to you a formal invitation to attend this evening's Honeysuckle Festival celebrations inside his palace. Enclosed with this letter is a pass that will inform the guards of your privileged status. His lordship hopes to see you and toast to your health tonight. In addition to this, the Baron requests that a number of your performers be brought to the estate as well for the entertainment of himself, his family, and his guests. Have you any questions?"

"Yes, how long did it take to memorize all that, hm?" Bumblefeld responded, twirling his mustache with a cheeky grin.

The emissary rolled his eyes. "Do you have any *relevant* questions, mister Bumblefeld?"

"Well not for someone so rude." The carnie stood, flicked his waistcoat behind him, and snatched up a cane. "You may inform the Baron's palatial manager that I shall make an appearance tonight if it pleases his lordship so much, *and...*" he began whacking the emissary with the stick of the cane all the way out of the tent, "you may inform him that I come in hope that not all of his staff speak to his lordship's guests with such incredulity! A good day, sir!"

The emissary scurried away back up the hill. Bimblewald looked at the giant now standing outside the top, holding a little hat in his hands and bowing his head low. "Why didn't you tell me I had a visitor before letting him in, Big Jack?"

"'e... 'e... 'e 'ad nife clofes." Big Jack stuttered out before starting to cry. "I'm sorry, mithter Bimble!"

"Ah, now, Big Jack. Don't cry. Just let me know next time, if you please." Bimblewald stretched and yawned. "I was having a fair dream before that rude awakening."

Bimblewald returned to his tent and sat at his desk trying to conjure the feelings he'd had seeing his wife again in his dreams. It was fruitless. Consciousness had long built up an immunity to such feelings in the interest of sanity, of 'moving on.' Now, only his dreams afforded the sad carnie the chance to experience happiness in memorial. He pulled a flask from his waistcoat and took a shot from the absinthe within to soothe his nerves.

4.

Donard sat his hammer down and looked out the window from the forge. The sun was beginning its western descent, telling the soot-faced dwarf it was time for an afternoon pipe. He walked out of the shop and crossed the lawn to his house, taking a moment to wash his face and hands in a fountain of running water built into the stone wall of his dwelling. High-quality smithing was a decent business that afforded him a number of small luxuries here in Verdendale.

Donard's true wealth, however, would never and could never be made by smithing. The world was advancing past the lone metalworker. Large mechanical foundries capable of casting in a day more than Donard could do in a week were popping up all along the Kuedino's major tributaries. This had long ago pressed Donard to focus more on local work or contracts that required a finer touch.

Some jobs paid much and others little, but Donard had made do for years before the foundries encroached closer and closer to Verdendale with their cheap products. Rather than give up on his long time trade, Donard instead became involved in other more clandestine means of supplementing his income. No more than three years passed, he'd been approached by a small group of less-than-savory characters who'd offered him gold in exchange for ... illegally obtained 'goods.'

Mostly, these 'goods' were specifically requested in a coded list of around four or five items mailed to him each week. Sometimes, they were 'goods' from households within the town and other times, they were from the surrounding area. The nature of the 'goods' ranged from intelligence to valuables, and even sometimes people though Donard had made a point to decline anything regarding slavery to which his contacts, who'd responded that they were not interested in slavery as much as extracting ransoms or information.

Regardless, the dwarf's work as a thief had gone on rather smoothly in that time. The robberies hadn't gone unnoticed, in fact the papers often headlined with his latest scores, dubbing him the "Green Valley Swiper." He thought that name lacked gravitas, but no one in town would have ever expected him of being the Green Valley Swiper, and he usually went by unnoticed. People often got uncomfortable seeing him due to his dwarfism, so they were more than willing to find something else to do, a fact Donard used to his advantage.

This week, a letter *had* come but did not have a detailed list of 'goods' to acquire. Rather, this week the letter only had one message: *On the night of the Honeysuckle Festival, enter Baron Balteshezzar's estate and ploy your trade. After you've obtained as much 'goods' as you can carry, leave the town and meet with our fence upriver. They will provide you just compensation depending on the 'goods' and our employment of your services will be concluded.*

Donard didn't quite know why his employment with the shady unnamed group was coming to an end, but he knew that if tonight *was* his last night, he was going to get as great a payout as possible and leave the smithing business for good. He hoped that if he made enough from tonight's haul, he'd be able to afford a new home in the caldera far removed from the schemes and failings of the industrial world.

He'd begin his work soon enough. For now, he waited on his front porch, watching the people make their way toward the Circus down the hill. He pulled a shining bronze pocket watch from his trousers and checked the time: two o'clock, on the dot. The grand performance would be starting in the big top in a couple of hours, which meant he had plenty of time to do a little extra work around the village.

Of course, the list only specified acquiring 'goods' from the palace, but the letter also said he'd be meeting a fence. What sort of fence would turn down the valuables of some relatively well-off townsfolk?

5.

Ifra took a seat in a chair by a window in the laboratory. She'd spent all day using what little ingredients she had in the concoction of medicines she thought might come in handy this afternoon. She'd formulated several vials of a mild pain-numbing agent and procured a selection of wines that had been deemed "unfit for consumption" for use as antiseptics. She mixed water, Mercury, and Palo Santo oil in a glass jar and dropped a number of surgical tools within to disinfect them. After that, she'd set up her machines and tools about the sparse counter space of the room, and now she sat surrounded by the machinations of her life's work, the study of the organism.

Ifra looked at the bookshelves surrounding the far side of the room. They were mostly unadorned save for a few pieces of literature her predecessor had left in his haste. She rose from her seat by the window and approached. Here was a book concerning the humors, there was one detailing the function of the human heart and blood. Then, a text on the bone structure of the human body, and beside it an edition of Professor V. L. Celebran's "Theory on the Separation of Soul and Body."

This one intrigued Ifra. She'd never been much concerned with the musings of occultists, with magic or spirits. However, if the soul was empirically studied, then it would prove most important for understanding the anatomy of organisms bearing it and so perhaps this thesis was worth a cursory read.

The author began by defining the soul and body: "The soul is an aspect of the human mind that allows them the phenomenon of "self actuality," the state of comprehending one's own existence beyond the base physical necessities of survival and reproduction. The soul is constituted by the individual unconsciousness. The Body

24

is a complex temporal shell through which the soul experiences time and space, both by controlling the unconscious machinations of organ operation (such as the pumping of the hard, or the ability to walk bipedally) and through the generation of conscious thought via the brain." Ifra stopped to contemplate these categories then continued.

In a later chapter, the professor elaborated on how the soul is housed in the mind. This is where the thesis took a turn away from academia and more along the lines of occultism. Celebran claimed that the soul did not exist corporeally, or at least that it was not limited by time and space, but instead was connected to all other souls by what could be imagined as an ethereal sea wherein all living beings dwelt simultaneously. The rest of the chapter was largely philosophical in nature, or at least Ifra thought so and skipped it.

Afterwards, Celebran detailed a hypothetical operation of the soul in relation to magic, stating that the mind chronicled information for the soul's use in producing behaviors and beliefs. This was controversial to Ifra as the professor's theory proposed a non-anatomical purpose to the brain never previously explored by any respectable medical scholars. Even the most learned physicians had only been able to discern a connection between the body and mind through certain structures: the spine, the eyes, the senses, and the humors.

This was an entirely new form of study all by itself. Even if the professor was wrong in his assertions or his methodology, it could compel scholars to conduct more research on the brain, perhaps even the formulation of a field of science entirely focused on its study. Ifra was deeply intrigued by this prospect and continued reading.

Ifra skipped forward to a section in the book where the professor detailed his own personal research into the deteriorations of the Mind and Soul. The scholar had observed many mentally ill patients and attributed madness to certain failed operations of the brains, affirming this upon close examination of the organs upon the subjects' deaths. However, the professor had also conducted tests and cross-examined sources from previous eras to determine that even an entirely healthy mind can be driven to certain forms of madness by the deterioration of the soul.

This, Professor Celebran determined, was the result of what he called "Necromancy." According to the scholar's findings, Necromancy directly deteriorates the Soul, either by destroying an individual's sense of self or sense of connection to the aforementioned "ethereal sea" depending on whether the spell is powered by the elimination of one's own Soul or that of another's. Ifra skipped over a lengthy discussion on what the author called the "Laws of Magic," as the idea of validating such unfalsifiable claims through assignment of structure seemed to further draw the whole thesis into question.

Down the page, Celebran detailed several experiments involving practitioners of occult sorcery to test his hypothesis. He found that the traditional understanding of Necromancy as the magic sourced by and effective in the manipulation of dead humorous material wasn't quite accurate. His assertion was that all magic was powered by destruction of the soul and that its effects on both subjects and objects could be varied and pervasive.

Finally, Celebran outlined in his conclusions on necromancy and souls that those affected by magic may display signs of various types of madness. He stated that even being in proximity to a particularly active sorcerer could begin to deteriorate the soul through an infectious disease he called Lich Sickness. In the end, Celebran determined that the destruction of the soul was mostly the effect of a sorcerer drawing power for a spell of some kind.

Ifra had read enough and put the book back on the shelf. While initially interesting, she found the points concerning sorcery and such to be more tedious than the professor's more anatomical observations. The doctor felt quite safe from evil witches and warlocks here in Verdendale. Over the past few decades, most of the occult had been snuffed out, leaving the only magicians on the frontier as little more than illusionists peddling card tricks.

While Ifra herself had no disdain toward magical use, her people had a deeply entrenched tradition of rituals and rites, she was not uncomfortable with the notion of more grounded scientific pursuits being sponsored by humanity, even if it was at the expense of the arcane. As she understood it, the Empire had done an adequate job of archiving all resources of occult literature while maintaining their enforcement of laws regarding its practice, so the knowledge would always be there even if practice became more scientific.

The doctor rose from the seat she'd taken while reading and decided to walk the grounds before they became swarmed with townsfolk.

6.

Bimblewald drew a golden pocket watch from his waistcoat to check the time with the last of the evening sunlight that shone through the canvas of the Big Top. The minute hand flicked over a quarter till six o'clock. Perfect timing.

He stepped out into the circuit as the performers were making their way out. He held up his cane with a grandiose flourish, pivoting upon his feet to bow before the crowd of cheering customers. "The sun sets behind the mountains in the west as yet another Honeysuckle Festival celebratory performance of Cirque du Grand Empris comes to a close! People of Verdendale, are you entertained?" The crowds cheered and happily tossed bits of flowers and kettle corn.

"I and my fellow performers wish to bid you a night of mirth and merriment, as the warm summer days approach. We thank you for your attendance and humbly wish you a gay evening!" Bimblewald took off his top hat and bowed once more toward the audience. After a brief moment, he rose, replaced his hat upon his head, and twirled in an about-face to exit the circuit.

Once through the tent flap that led to the outer ring of the big top, he made his way past the carnies removing their costumes and stowing the tools of their various performances in the crates. Walking outside the big top into the cool evening breeze, he heard a gleeful voice call, "Dada! Dada!" He turned to see a face as beautiful as his wife's gliding toward him, arms out as if they'd catch wings and fly.

"My darling, Esmerelda!" He picked the little girl up in his arms and kissed her auburn head. Her hair certainly smelled as if it needed a wash but he didn't quite care. "How was the show, my love?"

"Tonight's show was the best of the whole year, dada!" She smiled a grin that missed a few teeth, most of which remaining were adult chompers.

"I'm so pleased you enjoyed it, Esmerelda." He sat her back down on her feet and pulled the letter out of his waistcoat. "Unfortunately, I won't be able to stay for the stories tonight. The *Baron's* called me to his estate for the evening." He said, prompting them to both roll their eyes and parrot, "Ugh! Barons!" in a unified tone of disdain.

Bimblewald hugged his daughter close, "You'll tell me all the scary ones won't you?"

"Of course, dada." The girl said with an exaggerated salute.

Bimblewald's heart swelled as he looked upon his daughter, stunned by her mother's blue eyes. She was everything to him, and everytime he left her drew a sinking feeling to his gut. "Why don't you go find Patch and Valentino for me? Tell them to come to my tent with whatever they need for an impromptu performance." Esmerelda ran off and Bimblewald looked after her in adoration.

"She's a good lass." He heard a familiar brogue accent say behind him.

He turned to a middle-aged woman covering her leotard in a fur-lined robe. "Yes, a gold-standard if I do say so myself. Her mother would be proud."

"I know *I* am." The woman sauntered over to him and wrapped her arms around one of his. "Her father ain't so bad either." Bimblewald chuckled and laid a hand over her interlocked fingers. She looked up at him and pulled off the tight net holding her hair up, allowing her fiery locks to cascade down over one side of her face and his shoulder. "Lovely show, Mister B?"

"It was an amazing performance. *You* were amazing." He looked at her, saw the joy and longing in her heavy gaze. Then, a pang of remorse welled up within him and an apology filled his eyes. "Delilah, I..." He struggled to find the words to accompany his gentle removal of her hands from his arm. Instead he just cleared his throat and said, "... I have to go to the Baron's estate tonight. Will you look after Esmerelda, after storytime is over?"

She blushed at his touch, whether out of frustration or attraction Bimblewald couldn't tell, then brushed her hair to the side saying, "Will I? Sure, I'll put her to bed and see to it that the others get the tents all packed up for tomorrow."

"Please do, my dear. The riverboat captain has us leaving just after dawn tomorrow. We can't be late." He pulled the little flask from his coat and unscrewed the lid.

Delilah put her hand over the flask before it reached his mouth. "Far be it from me to tell a man not to drink, but you think they'll have enough up there with the 'big hats,' aye Mister B?" Her eyes met his with a mixture of empathy and dominance.

Bimblewald frowned at her, and screwed the lid closed. "Yes, you're probably right. I don't suppose absinthe and wine would mingle well anyways."

"No. No it wouldn't, Mister B. That stuff's mighty hard for an ordinary night, and you've had a bit too much for many ordinary nights now." She lifted his chin, drawing his eyes from the flask onto her. "C'mere to me, Mister B... she ain't in there, love. Maybe it makes the dreams more real, but it'll never bring her back."

At first, Bumblefled felt an old anger spark in him, but he'd gotten tired of being angry, especially at the other members of the Cirque. Instead, he choked a bit and some tears fell as he looked into Delilah's kind face. "I know." He said, shaking the tears away and clearing his throat of sorrow. "It's just a bad habit is all."

"Yer not so banjaxed as some of the other tools I've seen." the woman grinned at him, warming away his loss. For a moment, tears welled up in her own eyes as she saw the aching need for a drink in Bimlewald's eyes, but she knew he was trying at least. "Aye now, get crackin', the lords and ladies await. I'll tend to everything down here."

Octavian thanked her with a kiss on the hand and walked away to his tent. Inside, after a brief moment of thought, he took a swig from his flask. Bad habits don't easily die, least of all by admonition.

7.

The townsfolk were now beginning to come back from the Circus, which was perfect as Donard had just stashed his pickings from their houses. He'd decided upon a course of action he'd never have done in any other circumstances than his own departure from Verdendale. Tonight he'd targeted his own neighborhood.

The area was neither especially poor nor affluent. Mostly, it was shops containing commodities delivered via the river. There was a jewelry store, a bookshop, a luthier, and a boutique. The jewelry store was of course his first stop, better to make the most of his time safe from discovery robbing the most valuable commodities. Then, he went to the boutique, stealing a few pairs of expensive shoes and a number of nice hats. Next, a stop at the luthier to steal a rather fancy looking violin.

Finally, just before sounds of the people being released from the Big Top reached him, Donard visited the local printer. The 'goods' after all hadn't always been valuables. Sometimes, information was just as profitable, and though the printer mostly produced news that his buyers would most likely be aware of already, the larcenous smith thought that perhaps something hidden in the printer's notes could be worth a few bucks to the fence he was to meet.

He'd broken into the printing house without a hitch. His lockpicking skills had become quite tuned over the years, enough to break into a heavily secured jewelry shop let alone this small press. Once inside he'd hurried to the back of the building past the large press and into the printer's office. Immediately, he began rummaging through the journals that filled the drawers of the printer's desk.

He skimmed the pages, scanning for headings he thought were important. There was a journal regarding the town's troubles with 'native brigands.' Such things were old news, people expected to hear about that. Donard carefully replaced the journal in its place in the drawer.

One journal detailed the political orations of Lord Brigmond. Most of it was either outdated or mundane, yet one page recorded knowledge from one of the printer's informants that the Prime Minister was soon to announce the annulment of the Native Relocation Provision. While Donard was no activist, he'd become aware of certain important matters during his clandestine work. The Provision was signed by the United Baronies several a little less than a century ago to establish a sanctuary for natives in the aftermath of the Battle of the Broken People.

The battle was a major military victory for imperial forces which routed the largest alliance of Native tribes to date. The alliance dissolved after the battle allowing imperial soldiers to surround the disparate tribes and force them into work camps. Eventually, the Parliamentarians drafted the Provision, granting a small archipelago of islands off the colonial mainland to the Natives who wished to remain separate from the colonies. Natives unable to work, or who'd served in the Imperial Army, were "suggested" to migrate there, while most of their able-bodied kin were forced to remain in the work camps.

The islands in the Provision were large and tropical. For a while the exiles attempted to rebuild their society according to precedence set by the aforementioned alliance. All while under the strict observance of Imperial soldiers. As Donard understood, these efforts were going quite well for them up to this point.

The First-Nations Isles, as the provided sanctuary was called, had been an establishment for two generations, but as of late, tensions had risen between the Baronies and the Natives on account of Brigmond's policies regarding religious practices. The Natives of the Isles had proven resolute in codifying and protecting their different tribal traditions, which had brought trouble on them when the new Prime Minister had instituted an inquisition on anything resembling sorcerous or occultic practice.

Many of the First Nation's practices were all too alien to the heads of this inquisition, and thus all too easy to categorize as occultic. Trouble was, the Natives weren't keen on giving up their hereditary traditions on the order of imperial lords with no authority over them under the pact of the Provision. According to this printer's source, the prime minister was quite willing to demolish the peace established by his predecessors in order to further the goals of his inquisition.

Donard ripped the related pages from the notebook and folded them up. Stuffing them in his pocket. The time for larceny was over and he had to make his way home to stash his loot and prepare for the evening's *festivities*. Thus, he did and now he sat outside his house smoking another pipe full as he watched the people saunter merrily up to the estate, all of them eager to imbibe their lord's wine and gorge themselves on his harvests. Donard harrumphed to himself at the thought.

He was no brown-noser of lords and ladies. He had no love for the high and mighty, whose wealth and titles he thought were nothing but very elaborate covers not so dissimilar to his own as a smith. They were thieves no different than himself, surely. The only difference was that they'd convinced their victims that their theft was legal.

Yet, on the other hand, Donard watched as the humans of every class besides the rich indulged in this celebration of their own suffering and wondered how much better they were. Clever lords engaged in robbery, but the fools they'd robbed seemed quite pleased to finally enjoy the sweat of their brows despite the meager portions it was being served back to them in.

He watched farmers go to eat only a fraction of the bread their grain had produced, same for the huntsmen, the vinters, and the brewers. The smiths ate once a year with the silverware they'd made and the glaziers drank once a year from the glasses they'd crafted. To Donard, the fools were no more deserving of respect than the nobles. He saw through this ruse and decided that the ultimate act of defiance was to show these folk their folly. To rob them all blind and show them that to a force such as he, they were all equal.

He went inside, garbed himself in clothes that were nice enough to pass the gate guards but still comfortable enough to move in, covered it all in a darkly colored cloak, and proceeded up the hill to the palace. So engaged was he in his thoughts that he forgot his dagger upon a counter top in his kitchen.

8.

Ifra had been walking the palatial grounds for about three or four hours, and every second was necessary to explore the vast gardens surrounding the home of the baron. The building now shone a pale honey color in the burning hues of sunset, and the colors of the many gardens had become washed with that bittersweet lens of day's end.

The estate itself was built in a rather baroque style, facing south to catch both morning and evening light perfectly. Its foreground was an aisle of paved walkways dotted with statues of marble and bronze statues of idyllic champions, grotesque monsters, and dainty women. The north was a large mostly empty lawn save for a couple of fountains, trees, and a gazebo in its heart. One of the trees had a wooden swing dangling from a high limb by two ropes.

To the west was a grand hedge maze. Topiaries surrounded and filled the maze, making it a lovely place to get lost in. One never knew what the next verdant idol would look like and this gave the entire maze a mystical feel, as if the shrubs were forming themselves just beyond one's senses to delight the diligent explorer who found them.

Finally, the eastern flank of the grounds was dominated by botanical gardens displaying flora from across the world. Little rivers had been carved into the hilltop and ran water pumped in from deep underground to the myriad of decorative gardens. Several ponds were scattered throughout the scenery, providing homes for aquatic flora and fauna. Within the gardens, the world seemed to hum with the din of insects, amphibians, and birds. This harmony of life was kept perfect by the meticulous efforts of specialized teams of groundskeepers in the Baron's employ.

The gardens filled Ifra's sense of smell with overwhelming stimulation. By far this area of the grounds was her favorite, but now that only a bleeding edge sunlight illuminated the horizon, she began to feel uneasy. Something about the fleeting beauty of the gardens dissolving into shades of a single homochromous rust made her nervous, as if the whole world was decaying before her eyes. The slow but inevitable march of time would soon consume the sights and sounds of the gardens with oily shadow, or if they were lucky, cold moonlight.

Regardless, Ifra was powerless to stop the turning of the heavens, and thus quickly made her way inside where she was promptly approached by the Majordomo. "Ah, Doctor. I was just coming to inform you that we'll be starting the tour for the Baron's honored guests soon. Join us in the foyer if you please." The man turned for a moment as if to walk away, then looked back at Ifra with a furrowed brow. "Are you alright, Doctor? You look... worried."

Ifra looked back outside and realized that she had been moving a little faster than she thought. "Worried?" she cleared her throat and said, "No. I'm not worried. Just nervous for the festival."

"Ah, well in that case, you have nothing to fear. The Baron keeps a firm grip on law and order in this place. You won't be held responsible for the outcomes of any rowdiness this evening." This did not assuage her concerns. Nevertheless, Ifra nodded and followed the Majordomo through the halls to the foyer where a large group of people dressed in opulent clothing waited just down the stairs from the mezzanine.

In the foyer between the ground and the mezzanine railing hung a portrait of the Baron and his family hung as a centerpiece to the room. "This painting was composed by Tatiana V'Amarithusky two years ago in the solar room of the palace on the third floor. The boy on the left of the foreground is the Baron's youngest son, Thomas Balteshezzar, and to his right is the eldest, Marcus."

"The left in the background is the Baron's wife, Mélanie Delusión de Dureaux of the Setchevali Vale of Durantia. In her arms is the youngest child and only daughter, Leona Balteshezzar, who at the time of its painting was two years old. Finally, on the right of the background is the High Baron himself, Lord Vincent Balteshezzar."

The group then moved on from the foyer into the western wing of the ground floor where they were introduced by the Majordomo to the lobby. "In the daylight," their guide explained, "this room is brightly lit through its glass outer walls. Sunrays gleam off of the suits of armor collected over the years and stationed along the eastern wall. The sofas and armchairs here are all cushioned to feel as if one were seated on the clouds. Please note that during the festivities, this room as well as the foyer and the next room we'll be visiting will be the permitted rooms for mingling."

Then from the lobby, they walked through a northern door into the Gallery. Throughout the room, free standing walls created a criss-cross pattern, all covered in various pieces of art and archeology. Some walls were set with shelves displaying artifacts of native culture from antiquity all the way to items from the current diaspora. On the next wall hung paintings of conflicts between the natives and the colonists, portraits of famous generals that had fought to advance expansion over the Frontier.

This exhibition of the sorry state of this country's native peoples was uncomfortable for Ifra. By the way these "nobles" spoke about the natives, she was quite sure that if given the chance, they'd revel in the opportunity to glory over her country too, and in fact had in centuries past when her homeland was annexed into their "great and glorious" empire. She would have liked to believe otherwise but the words of the chamberlain from earlier that day made her doubtful.

Finally, the group departed from the gallery through a set of double doors upon the northern wall. They entered into a gilded hall that ran the entire length of the palace. "This," said the Majordomo, "is the Sunset Hall. The Balteshezzar's wished for a chamber on the ground floor that would capture the hues of the evening light as beautifully as the exterior of the palace does." Golden plating actuated everything in the room, from the reliefs along the southern wall depicting numerous myths in the Imperial religion's canon to the pillars ordered with a style that was reminiscent of the forest canopy.

Every hue of the dying light of day reflected off the surfaces of the hall with such brilliance that it made one forget the mundanity or anxiety of nightfall, replacing the feeling with a sense of romance. The room was immersed in sunset hues and the beauty of it all put everyone in the room in a state of relaxation. After a moment of quiet mingling, servants entered the hall bearing trays of Honeysuckle Mead.

The majordomo lifted his voice of the crowd saying, "Guests of the Baron, at this time, you may take your first taste of his lordship's bounty. Help yourself as the wine-bearers make their way around the room." Ifra took a glass and sipped, sensing the distinct floral bouquet almost immediately. The mead was quite sweet, a bit too much for her tastes but the balance of the honeysuckle flavor underpinning the ambrosial taste was invigorating.

Just then, a couple approached Ifra who seemed to be already quite inebriated. "Oh my! You have such lovely skin." the woman proclaimed a bit too loudly, "You must be from the east, yes?"

Ifra held back her indignance, "Yes, ma'am. I am from Khuttania."

"Ah! That accent, almost as smooth as the mead. So exotic!" The airiness of the woman's tone was grating. Her golden hair was in a high round bulb over her head, so loosely held in place that when she moved about in her drunken manner, the dressing would bounce about like a tulip bulb in the wind. "Grissom! She half-twirled to her husband, "Grissom we simply must plan a trip to Khuttania."

The man looked at her, obviously perturbed. "Deleanor, we really should be going, the lord's of Greysborrow and Kolgrim are here and I have..."

"Grissom, don't be such a grouch." The woman looked back at Ifra, saying with a grin that seemed just a bit too wide, "My husband is a very industrious man, always so consumed with business and politics that he barely notices I exist most days." She then barked a sound that might have been a laugh if it didn't sound so fake.

"Oh it's quite alright, miss. If he has business to attend to then perhaps it's best you be off." Ifra responded in an attempt to escape the couple's presence.

"Indeed," the husband finally seemed to take notice of Ifra, "now come along, Deleanor."

"Now wait just a minute, I still have questions." The woman pulled her arm out of the man's grip, inciting a baleful stare from her husband. "I simply must know something. We hear so much from Khuttania. One thing has always fascinated me but my husband's business rarely allows him to travel beyond the Baronies and this may be my only chance to get some answers. Miss, you must tell me, what exactly goes on at a 'harem?'"

"A harem, ma'am?" Ifra asked incredulously.

"Deleanor! That's hardly appropriate to speak about in fine company." The husband growled through gritted teeth.

"Hogwash, Grissom! You and the mayor of Athelsberry spoke about harems over cigars and scotch just last month. I seem to remember hearing the two of you fawn over the concept rather fondly." With that, the husband's face flushed and his mouth shut. "Now, please, you must tell me what happens at these events, miss. I'm dying to know." Deleanor said looking back at Ifra.

"Ma'am, I don't know what you've heard but I…"

The woman sensed Ifra hesitance and interjected. "Come now, don't keep secrets! It must be glamorous, and…" she bit her lip and blushed, "well, sensual so I hear."

Ifra grit her teeth and pursed her lips, "Ma'am, as I was saying, I don't know what you've heard, but it isn't accurate. It is a cultural practice for families, and far from being sensual, is in fact mainly kept for the sake of modesty."

"Oh, keep your secrets then." Deleanor responded, much to Ifra's confusion. "The truth is in the details, miss. Deny it if you must, but the people who've told me the details of these harems are well informed. Too bad, I had thought to host a harem at my estate on the coast this summer, perhaps you could have come." She winked at Ifra, whose own expression had morphed to something between confusion and indignity.

"That's enough, Deleanor!" With that, her husband practically dragged the woman away, leaving Ifra desperately holding her composure, gripping her wine glass tightly. When at last she was able to once again form coherent thoughts, all she could say to herself was, *This is going to be a long night.*

9.

Bimblewald looked himself up and down in a tall mirror sitting on the ground. His tent was illuminated only by a gaslamp on his desk. He'd dressed himself as well as he could for the evening. Nice enough for a ball, but simple enough to be inexpensive. He wasn't aiming to turn any heads tonight anyways.

"Miphter Bumble, Pash and Valentino are outphide." Octavian heard his doorman say. He called for them to enter and in walked Patch the Jester and Valentino "the Magnanimous Magician!"

Patch was dressed in a fool's cap with two drooping points adorned with brass bells. He was a thin man and his face showed his age by its abundance of wrinkles and liver spots. On his hip hung three masks, the first of which was a basic jovial facade for the expression of foolish behavior. The second was white with a smiling red mouth and black dots that Patch used for laughing gestures when the audience was the butt of a joke, while the third mask was red with a black frown and white dots when Patch himself was the butt of a joke. The old clown was very proficient at playing a crowd even though his age had begun to limit his range of motion.

Valentino was quite the opposite of old Patch. He was young and attractive, a fact that had gotten the circus in trouble a number of times when one of his "tricks" involved intimacy with a local of whatever given town they were performing near. Indeed, his talents as an illusionist were quite valuable and had been the final motivation for Bumblefeld's defense of the boy when all his patience was gone.

He had thin mustaches, seperated in the middle and shaved to sit just in between his lip and nose, and his hair was long and sleek underneath the large beret he wore. He'd dressed himself in an older style of clothes that he

42

said made him seem, "beyond time." This consisted of a white shirt with frills around his cuffs and neck beneath a black overshirt wrapped by a mid-length black and gold cape, tight black spanks, and knee high boots.

"Esmerelda told us to be ready for a performance." Valentino said.

"Right. The baron has requested that I attend the celebrations in the estate tonight and that I bring a couple of performances for his guests. I decided that your acts would be appropriate for the occasion. Have you everything you need?"

"I wish I would have known! I'd have brought my sheep skins." Valentino grinned lecherously and Patch rolled his eyes.

"None of that tonight, my boy, please. Do you have everything you need?" The two of them nodded and the three began to leave the circus grounds when Esmerelda ran to her father and the two embraced.

"You'll have fun, won't you dada?" She asked.

"Perhaps so, Ezzy. You know how crowded these things can be."

"You love crowds though."

"Not these kinds." Bimblewald said as his thoughts flicked to days past with the girl's mother. They'd attended many a ball and banquet together, and she'd always been the comforting hand that settled his nerves among the nosey and gossiping noble types.

"I think it'll be nice." She mused on and on about all the exciting things to do at parties, drawing a loving grin to Octavius' face.

"I love you more than anything in this world, darling." He hugged her and smiled warmly. "Now, go and listen to Dehlila's stories. I'll be back soon." She nodded and he set her back on the ground, letting her run back towards the tents. Then, the three carnies set off toward the estate for the evening.

10.

Both the estate and its grounds were well and truly swarmed with people. Townsfolk and travelers alike were all generating a boisterous din of social jabberwocky. The noise filled the air like a swarm of bees hovering over Donard's head. The dwarf had made his way past the palace gate and taken a seat on a table strewn with an absurd amount of food.

He grabbed a turkey leg and slapped it onto a plate along with a handful of potatoes and buttered rolls. As he was eating and drinking a mug of cider, a dirty-looking man fell next to him on the bench. "'Ella there, harflin'. You 'ere fer the loot too, am I right?"

"I don't know what you're talking about. I'm just trying to eat a decent meal before the night's done." Donard said, keeping his eyes to his food. He looked up only briefly with a dark visage and stated, "It's best you go on and do the same."

"Ah!" the stranger wagged his finger at Donard. "I know the look of a rascal when I see one, do I, an' you're one of 'em, hard right! I can't be wrong, I can't. You been eyein' the guards since ya got through the gate, you 'ave! What're ya spying, eh? I got me eyes on 'at lass o'er there, I do."

Donard looked toward where the man was pointing. There stood a nice-looking young woman that couldn't be more than twenty years old. He observed her dress. It was nice, much nicer than it looked like the stranger could afford, but it wasn't the dress of a woman that carried a coin purse with her. Several signs of wear showed that the dress was most likely a hand-me-down that had been repaired by a moderately talented seamstress over the years. He'd say that the woman's entire dowry couldn't have been more than forty silver. His attention returned his focus back to the man.

44

"Oh, I'll have 'er, I will. I don' right care if she even 'as a single coin on 'er, I don't. I'll 'ave her anyways, anyhows." He laughed mischievously at Donard.

The dwarf, filled with rage, slammed his fist on the table and the thought crossed his mind to bury his dagger in the man's chest that very second. Donard was a burglar, but he at least considered himself an honest one. This fool was a bandit, a low-down amateur with no class, no skill, and no dignity.

But then, the old smith had an idea that might solve several problems at once. He stood up and walked away, making sure to lose the man's attention in the crowds, then approached the guards at the gate. They were garbed in their ceremonial uniforms: black coats with colorful ribbons and sashes, matching trousers, and leather boots, all topped by a tall dark helmet adorned with a star in the center of the forehead. Lettering in the center of the eight-pointed star read, "Verdendale City Police." Each had a baton on one hip and a revolver on the other. "You there, police! You've a problem, I tell you." Donard said, approaching the nearest one to himself.

"What is it, dwarf?" one of the officers asked diminutively.

"I think you've got yourself a lecherous scalawag just over there making threats against the Baron's guests."

"What sort of threats?" the officer asked with only the slightest interest.

"Threats against her." Donard indicated the woman in question. "He was making quite the case against himself for intending her defilement. I thought perhaps the Baron's guard dogs would be interested in the defense of his lordship's guests."

The officer took a look at the woman Donard had pointed towards and shrugged, saying, "Well, if the lecherous dolt intends to defile anyone, I'd say he picked the right one." Both of the officers laughed mischievously.

Donard's eyes filled with indomitable fury and he was about to ask what sort of policeman this man thought he was before the other one spoke up. "Away with you, dwarf! We'll inform the next patrol to pass of your suspicions and they'll handle it. The Baron's guests won't be facing any abuse tonight. Now go on and enjoy the evening, it *is* the Honeysuckle Festival after all."

Donard kicked the officer closest to him in the shin and stomped off with a fat spit, muttering to himself about the wicked dogs that allow such men to be called "protectors." He found himself a bench near the botanical gardens and took a seat to observe the patrols and look for a proper entrance to the estate. He'd only been sitting there for a moment when he noticed another darkly cloaked figure on a bench across the gardens from himself.

Each looked at the other for a moment as if to recognize that both knew whatever the other was up to wasn't quite legal. When the figure looked away without moving, Donard felt like it was a sign that he or she had no intention of getting in his way. He hoped he was right because he didn't have time to lose bantering with a rival burglar.

Just then, horns sounded from the front gate of the grounds and all the guests arranged themselves about the road to the estate's entryway. Donard stood and saw over the heads crowding townsfolk the tops of several decadent carriages glide toward the facade. The crowds raised their hands and cried, "Hail, Baron Balteshzzar! Hail, Lord Borguemont! Hail, the Rosary Inquisition!"

The last hail made the old smith's heart sink. He looked behind the carriages and saw a dozen and a half robed figures bobbing up and down on great shire horses. Mock kite shields hung from the creatures' flanks and Donard knew there was an array of deadly weapons underneath each one. These were the "paladins" of the Rosary Brotherhood. To the people, they were "monster-hunting, witch-killing protectors of the common folk standing against the dangers of wickedness." To Donard, they were yet another obstacle to acquiring the 'goods' he needed from the estate tonight. An obstacle the old smith feared more than any number of police officers the Baron could muster.

11.

Ifra watched as the affluent crowd of the Baron's guests ebbed and flowed about the enormous foyer, sipping fine wines and helping themselves to h'orderves delivered by roaming servants. One group let out an exclamation of coos as a magician finished some work of illusion, another group laughed pompously as a jester made a fool of himself and others. So far, the festivities were fairly tame.

The energy of the event became electric when the horns were heard outside. Everyone in the foyer moved away from the vestibule doors and opened a lane all the way to the stairs that climbed the mezzanine. When the doors opened, the entire crowd roared with applause as the Baron and his family entered the palace at last, followed closely by about a dozen men all in black and red robes. Colors, Ifra noted, which were distinctly out of theme for the evening.

The Baron was draped in the finest garments imaginable, such that had he not already become the premier signatory of the entire crowd's attention, he surely would have as he ascended the mezzanine stairs and stood central to the room. Ifra had never seen the man but she thought the portraits had done him credit. He was fit for his age, his hair still had some darkness to it and despite its ever-so-slight metallic color, showed no signs of thinning. His face was clean-shaven and wrinkled around the eyes and forehead, in addition to deep laugh lines that made his expression seem grim when he wasn't smiling.

Yet smiling he was as he reached his pedestal overlooking the crowd of wealthy guests in attendance tonight. He raised his hand to calm the applause. "What a pleasure it is to return from the capital to a place so beautiful as my home, Verdendale, at such a lovely time as the Honeysuckle Festival and among such esteemed guests." The crowds clapped again until the Baron held up his hand in a gesture for silence.

"My friends, these are… uncertain times. The world around us falls by the wayside. Ancient wisdom is discarded for the most deplorable cults of lunatics and murderers." The crowds hushed further into a breathless silence. "It is in these times that I, and I believe all our people, should be grateful to live in such a peaceful and prosperous province as these United Baronies of Alasthia." The crowd hailed in unison before the Baron continued. "Here, my friends, we are safe and secure. We are strong and free. I am proud to be a Baron of such loyal and faithful subjects as those that live in Verdendale. My family has been a guide and shield for her imperial majesty's expansion into these forests and hills that had been long wasted by primitive people. We have brought industry, we have brought security, and we have brought enlightenment behind us with every step.

"If I would be so bold, I would like to address something that I'm sure has affected you all. These native rabble that have so assailed us? You know them, and I must tell you that they do not represent their people. For two-hundred years now, the native folk of the frontier have lived in harmony with us. In Redder Valley, there are many settlements where our two races grow together without unrest and hatred.

"It is not their kind that causes them to rise up and exert violence upon the innocent. It is that single great evil that has corrupted the souls of human beings since the beginning, that evil which we barons have been working to annihilate in recent years. It is that evil for which the Prime Minister himself, Lord Brigmond…" all hailed, "lent his support to the Rosary Brothers, who make no mistake my friends, *are* the protectors of liberty and enlightenment. That evil is wicked, unholy witchcraft and it has beset our country to the very core."

As the Baron said this, a figure rose up the stairs to stand by his side. The stranger's black and red robes were adorned on the head with a tall almond-shaped hat all embroidered in gold and jewels. His face was covered by a metal mask resembling a lion with a third eye on its brow. Something deep inside the Ifra felt uneasy at the sight of the stranger. She felt as if from within her blood, her ancestors cried out against this man, growling through the eons from within primeval jungles.

"It is for this reason that it is my honor to introduce you all to the leader of the reconstructed order of clerics, the Grand Lion of the Rosary Brotherhood, Saint Ulrich the Enlightened!" All the people clapped and smiled, prompting Ifra to join out of propriety, but that sense of dread was no less potent.

"My children." The Vicar began with a voice like the creaking of a mausoleum gate, "The honor is mine to attend this celebration of life and beauty with such loyal and honest people around me. As I look upon your faces, I see such potential that my hopes are lifted. Any enemy of our liberties and our way of imperial life could not hope to stand against us. It is my mission to ensure that the people of this land are given the truth and are freed by that truth through our conduct. We must remain devoted to enlightenment and to our vigorous crusade against those who would use blasphemous sorcery against the knowledge of peace."

Even as she was a few feet behind the stranger, Ifra's nose prickled as the man's mouth spewed forth the scent of wine and... something else. Something like the smell of a cadaver during a dissection. It was as if the Lion's mouth was more like the maw of a tomb full of rotten corpses, and his words like the fragrance of exhumation.

"I believe," he continued, "that after tonight, I will be utterly convinced that the good people of Verdendale are

50

among the wisest and most devoted people to the cause among all the other Baronies." The crowd cheered and the High Baron bid that without further ado, the celebrations commence with the toast of the first glass of Honeysuckle Mead. After all in the crowd had been given a glass, they rose, the Baron drank first, then all others drank and entered into what Ifra thought was an abrupt change of pace from earlier in the evening.

After a moment of mingling, Ifra watched the Lion and the Baron disappear into the halls of the estate. She thought this odd but decided that her place was to ensure the health and safety of the Baron's family, who'd stayed in the foyer to mingle. Hence, the doctor kept her perch on the mezzanine and watched. All the while, the feeling of doom was not abated by the mead.

12.

"Are you Mister Bimblewald?" Octavius heard a young voice say.

He turned to see the little Miss Leona Balteshezzar staring up at him through blonde hair with bright eyes the color of mahogany wood. "Why yes, my lady, and you are the Baron's daughter if my eyes are correct." He smiled at her and got down on his knee, slowly to abate the pain in his joints.

"They are correct." The young lady said with propriety. "Don't call me by my father, though. I am Leona Balteshezzar. That is my name and I expect to be addressed by it, good sir."

Bimblewald bowed his head and intonated regret. "My deepest apologies, lady Leona. You certainly do deserve the honor. Can you forgive me?"

"I can, good sir. Let no one say that I am not merciful."

"Indeed, my lady, let no such words be uttered."

"Now, I have heard that you are the manager of that fine circus just outside the town, the one that comes every year. Is this true?"

"It is, my lady."

"I have also been informed that the children of the town are allowed to listen to stories while their parents celebrate the Festival."

"This is also correct, my lady."

"I would like to attend the story-telling this evening, if you please. These mongrels bore me and wish to be properly entertained."

Just as Bimblewald could respond, a woman pushed through the crowd in distress and shouted at the girl. "I apologize, sir. This one has a tendency to be unruly." the woman said. Bimblewald assumed she was Leona's caretaker or tutor.

"It's no trouble, ma'am. We were just having a rather cordial conversation about my circus. I'm sure you saw it on your way in."

"Ah, um, yes. We passed it." Leona attempted to rid herself of the woman's grip to no avail.

"My lady expressed distaste for the celebrations here in the estate and showed interest in attending the story-telling we have during the festivities. If it's all the same to the Baron, I surely wouldn't oppose her attende-"

"Absolutely not." The woman interrupted. "It is not proper, good sir."

"Oh, I meant no disrespect, ma'am. I only meant…"

"I'll hear no further discussion on this matter. Leona, we must go. The Osterian Duke's son is over here and he… " The woman rambled herself into a tirade of political jargon while Leona looked sadly back at Bimblewald. He wished there was something he could do for the young lady but Octavius well knew that the wealthy had a tendency, no perhaps more of a rule, to distance themselves from the activities of the lower classes. This systemic oppression of young minds was made infinite, indomitable, and increasingly violent in its cycle and, as Bimblewald looked after the little lady, he realized that hate would always exist so long as the young are not allowed to hear stories.

He was broken from his thoughts by a violent jerk backwards. He barely kept his feet on the ground as his assailant began frisking him. The nobleman's hand felt up and down Bimblewald's body until the old carnie pushed the fool off and fixed his outfit. "Good sir!" Octavius exclaimed, "are you demented?"

"Where's your gun?" the man shouted with a look of madness in his eyes.

"I don't have one!" Octavius responded.

"Bullshit! I demand a duel, sir! At once!" With that, the nobleman drew a pistol from an elaborate holster at his hip.

"I beg your pardon?" Octavius looked around for assistance, but few seemed to have even noticed what was taking place. In fact, the rest of the guests seemed to be as mad as the man before him. Partners danced wildly out of rhythm to the already discordant music. Glasses of wine clashed together so hard they shattered to the amusement of their handlers. Food flew from the dining room in the north wing as the men and women scrambled across the tables searching for some morsel that might satisfy their apparently ravenous appetites.

"Draw!" Bimblewald heard and jumped to the side just in time to miss a shot from his attacker. He launched himself to the ground to avoid another shot and quickly scrambled to his feet. Where were the guards? He looked to the vestibule door where two had been standing, but alas! They were gone.

The enraged nobleman continued his advance, forcing Octavius to stumble to the side once more. This time, the pistol gave the carnie a good cut across his arm. His waist coat began to turn red near the tear and Bimblewald decided it was high time he and his fellow carnies left.

Octavius ran from the madman who'd apparently only loaded three rounds and had to reload the weapon before firing again, which he struggled to do thanks to his shaky hands and uncontrolled laughter. "Patch! Valentino! It's time to leave!" The carnie called over the escalating sounds of scratching and arhythmic tones from the band.

Behind him, the madman had finally finished loading his weapon, causing Bimblewald to run through the crowd to the stairs of the mezzanine, gaining some time as the dancers gave the madman pause. Octavius watched him turn his pistol on the dancers, shooting them without hesitation as he continued demanding a duel. They delighted in the sight of their own blood. Anyone on the peripheries of the foyer began to laugh as well, and the madman bowed to them with a look of pride.

This was certainly not what Bimblewald had thought noble parties were like, and he'd quite decided he'd never attend one again when he ran into a pair of Rosary Brothers guarding the stairs. "Oh, thank heavens! Some lunatic just tried to murder me over there. I think he's killed a number of the guests. Please, you must help."

The hooded and robed clerics didn't move, and the dark holes where their eyes should have been imposed upon Bimblewald a feeling of malice and apathy. "Please, sirs!" He attempted to grab one of them and instantly felt his wrist turn in the most painful direction. He fell to his knees at the feet of the clerics and looked up at them in confusion. There they stood, staring at him. He looked into the darkness of the eyes behind their hoods but all Octavius could see was faint glints of ghostly light dancing in the shadows.

Bimblewald's heart began to race. He rose to his feet and backed away from the Brothers, turning his back to them only when he felt he was a safe distance. Spying through the crowd, his carnies were nowhere to be seen, nor could Octavius bring his nerves under control enough to really search for them. He just kept moving. Around all the frivolity and violence as the foyer churned with insanity.

The intoxicated dancing had turned into a blood orgy as wounded men drew knives and guns on each other while others began to engage in violent, scarlet-soaked sex. As Bimblewald finally made his way toward the dining room, a thought occurred to him: where was the young Leona in all of this?

13.

Donard was finished watching. The guard patrols hadn't passed by for a little under an hour since the Baron had arrived so he decided they'd been moved into the estate to deal with whatever commotion was going on in there. Given the racket, Donard guessed the whole place had devolved into a drunken brawl. The only guards the dwarf had seen on the grounds were about a half dozen of the dark-robed clerics.

Donard knew by reputation that the Rosary Brothers were nothing to scoff at but he felt pretty confident that he'd be able to avoid their notice. The only thing that gave him pause was the disappearance of the other figure he'd noticed. The darkly cloaked mystery man had moved off toward the southern grounds not long after the Baron's entourage had arrived.

That one knew Donard was here. In fact, the dwarf felt that he'd been the only one among the guests to really have observed him. He felt uneasy at the idea that whoever that one was had guessed his purpose here, but there was no time to hesitate. If he were going to get anything of value from the palace, he'd have to move now.

So he did. He began making his way into the botanical gardens, swift and silent. He ducked between bushes, statues, and trees, always making sure to have something between him and the estate *and* to keep a weather eye out for the clerics. He hadn't gone far before noticing a couple of the fiends marching about along the many paths through the gardens.

When he had a moment's peace, Donard took stock of all the entrances he could use. Windows were spaced out upon the palace in a regular pattern, but the only entrance on this side was a door into what appeared to be a greenhouse connected directly to the estate. Donard knew it'd give him access to the first floor. He could find his way to the upper levels once inside. There'd be less people in the upper levels, and more 'goods.' A perfect set-up for a good night's take.

Just then, Donard heard a shriek on his right. He looked and saw a familiar woman run from behind a line of tall bushes. It was the woman he'd seen in the crowd, the one that the revolting amateur had been ogling, and she'd been stripped of her outer garments. She ran toward him crying hysterically, until she tripped over a rather large tree root. Donard watched in horror as the lecherous oaf appeared from behind the bushes and dragged her back out of sight.

He ought to have known the guards wouldn't have dealt with that bastard son of a whore. Wherever they were, he hoped they were pleased with themselves and began running his way over to where he'd seen the woman and her assailant disappear. He didn't notice any of the guards or even the clerics around the western side of the grounds.

When he turned the corner around the bushes, he saw what the vermin was doing to the woman and flew into a rage. Everything was red hot adrenaline as he grabbed a large rock and attacked the girl's attacker until finally, his senses returned and he looked down at the man's head, bashed near a blood-filled pond. He looked about, disoriented from the fight, and saw the limp body of the young woman. She appeared to have attempted to crawl away, but hadn't made it very far.

A trail of blood soaked the ground from where she'd been defiled, and pooled between her legs. Donard stumbled over to her and turned her over. Her tongue had been bitten out, either by herself or by that madman he didn't know. Her face was locked in a permanent expression of sheer terror. Her eyes flicked to Donard before falling into a dead stare.

The dwarf's stomach turned and his mind swirled as he dropped her corpse and stumbled away from it. All he could do was move towards the door of the greenhouse. He didn't even know what he'd look for inside, he just knew he had to be somewhere else. Moving, numb and confused, he reached the door and tried to open it.

Unlocked? Why was it unlocked? He thought surely he'd have to pick the door but no, it was already open. His sense of caution seemed to sober his shock somewhat as he entered, making sure to observe his surroundings. Once inside and sure he was alone, he threw up in the corner and fell so tired he just wanted to fall and sleep after each step.

After making his way through the dark and comfortably warm greenhouse towards the door that he could only guess would let him into the estate proper, he heard a step. It was so soft he thought it might have just been in his mind, but no. When he turned to look where the step was coming from, he saw the cloaked figure crouched behind him.

Donard threw his elbow back to strike the stranger, but instead of the thud of his bone against the stranger's face, he felt his arm lift up, and his back leg give. Next thing he knew, Donard was on his back with a hand over his mouth and a blade to his throat. "Who are you?" a voice said from under the deep cowl.

The dwarf's shock was wearing off now, or was simply being subverted by his rage. He pushed the man's hand away and whispered, "That's none of your business."

"That remains to be seen. What exactly is *your* business here?"

"I can't say that's your business either, now get that blade off my neck or…"

"Or what?" The figure pressed the blade against Donard's skin just enough to cut a little.

The dwarf felt the trickle of his blood drip down his neck. "If there has to be introductions, all I'm tellin' you is that I'm here to relieve the Baron of some of his worldly possessions and that's it."

"Who do you work for?"

"I work for my damn self, that's who."

"I don't think so, but the fact that *you* do says something at least." The figure pulled back the cowl to reveal a native woman.

"What the hell are you doing here?"

"There is a great evil that's about to befall the people of this town. My people learned of it and I was hoping to change their fates, but it's too late now."

"Well I don't know nothin' about that, missy, so you can go on with your heroics and let me do my robbin' in peace."

"No! You must find a way to leave this place at once. There is a necromancer here and his curse will consume you if you don't leave soon. Every living soul has been feeding him power since he arrived."

"I can't leave. If I don't get this job done, I won't have the money to skip town, and if I don't skip town, I'll be hanged by the morning."

"Didn't you hear what I just said? There won't be a town tomorrow. You have to find a way off these grounds."

"What do you mean 'find a way?' The gates are just outside."

"I checked the gates to the grounds just a moment ago." She said grimly. "They've been locked shut by some sort of electric mechanism. It seems to only be opened by a certain type of key."

Donard cursed under his breath. "What about the clerics? They'd certainly be interested in helping hunt a loose warlock?"

"I'm not willing to gamble on the likes of them." *Fair enough,* Donard thought, *they'd likely just kill you on principle anyways.* The native continued, "If that's not what they're doing here already, then they may even be under his thrawl. Many of the townsfolk are, judging by their rabid behavior. I'm honestly quite surprised that you aren't displaying any signs of this influence." The eyes of the dead young woman flashed in Donard's memory, sparking a slight headache.

Just then, both of them heard the greenhouse door open and the deep thud of bootsteps slowly crossing through the rows of flora. The two of them went silent and Donard looked at his feet. They were covered in bloody mud, and he'd foolishly tracked his way into the greenhouse of the bodies outside.

The woman observed this and shook her head. "Go, find the key that opens the gate and get out of this place now." With that, she let go of Donard and stood, drawing a pistol from her side and firing, then she ran out the door leading the cleric in pursuit, allowing the dwarf to run through the opposite door into the estate.

14.

Ifra looked up from the giggling man whose wound she was applying pressure to. She needed a tourniquet, but the entire room seemed to have gone just as insane with no sign of the police guards. She couldn't leave the man to die, but with this level of blood loss, it was a certainty. Ifra cursed in frustration and ripped a long strip off the hem of her dress, double wrapping it high and tight on the man's thigh, just above the fatal gunshot wound that had been inflicted on him by another guest only moments ago.

She then pulled one of her hair pins out, made a windlass for the cloth, and twisted aggressively until the bleeding stopped. During all this, the patient had done nothing but laugh maniacally as his lifeblood poured freely onto the ground. He'd barely acknowledged the pain Ifra knew was common when applying a tourniquet.

With the bleeding stopped, the doctor finally looked up at the absolute delirium that had ensued in the foyer. All around her, people were fighting, slipping in pools of gore, and crying with pleasure. Ifra didn't know what to do and desperately searched the room for the majordomo or even the chamberlain?

"There you are, you miserable whore!" the doctor heard behind her. It was the nobleman and his wife from the sunset room, the former of which was holding his face in agony. When he reached Ifra, he lowered his hand to reveal his left eye deflated and dangling from its socket.

"Good doctor! My husband! His eye!" the woman cried.

"I must take him to my laboratory! Come!" she ushered them past the clerics who'd taken up guarding the mezzanine stairs with a disturbing sense of stoicism, and then through the hallways to her lab.

"Sit here, I'm going to give him an anesthetic. Something to dull the pain." She filled a small glass with the liquid and gave it to the man to drink. She went back to the desk, put on a pair of black rubber gloves that reached her elbows, then pulled her snips from the disinfectant.

Turning back to the patient, she was confronted by the woman. Her hair was let down, or rather ripped down, from its tall style. She sauntered over to her, the woman's visage now shifted into a menacing and lascivious grin. "My, my doctor. What a rush you're in to help my poor ailing *husband*." She spat the last word with some annoyance. "Perhaps we could just let him sit a while. I'm sure he'll get over it, doctor. I can think of many other things I'd rather do right now than watch you dote on him."

"Miss, I must remove your husband's eye or he'll be in constant pain. He could die if it goes on long enough, so please move aside."

She attempted to walk past her, holding her hands at eye level to avoid touching anything in the lab. When she got beside the woman, she put her hand on Ifra's breast. "What if I want him in pain, doctor? What if I like it?" The Doctor shot the woman a bewildered stare and tried to push past her again. Instead, the woman lowered her hand slowly, "What if I want to feel something new in life? Something much more... like you." With that the woman grabbed Ifra's crotch.

The Doctor dropped her snips and slapped the woman away, who backed up slightly then looked up at her with a grin, "Yes! Just like that! Do it again!" She charged at Ifra, who turned, grabbed the chair at her desk and swung it at the madwoman with all her strength. It hit her with a thud and she fell to the ground laughing and begging for more.

Ifra looked at the snips on the ground. *Can't use them now,* she thought and turned back to the desk, deciding she'd have to use the scalpel to remove the patient's eye. Then she felt a hand tighten around her ankle.

"Please!" the lunatic at her feet cried, "I must know what it feels like!"

She kicked her hand away and shimmied around her, "Ma'am, I have no idea what delusions have overtaken yourself and all the other guests, but I am a doctor not harlot and I have a job to do, so please just stand asi-"

She looked at the woman's husband sitting in his seat in the corner of the room. Somehow during the commotion, he'd gotten up and obtained a lobotomy pick from somewhere in the room. "You know bitch, it doesn't hurt. It feels good actually. I... I want to feel it again."

No, no, no! Ifra rushed to the man but was too late. He'd shoved the pick through his forehead and fallen limp. Behind, the doctor heard the woman rise giggling.

She turned and saw her with the snips in her hand. "I want it doctor, that body of yours. If you won't give it to me, I'll just take it." The woman rushed at her with the most deranged look.

Ifra moved aside, avoiding her stabs with the snips. Eventually, she exposed the back of her head to the doctor, and in a moment of pure instinct, shoved the scalpel deep into the base of her skull. The woman fell with a thud and convulsed on the ground for an eternity as the good doctor allowed herself a moment to embrace the confusion. Her eyes welled up in tears as she struggled to remove the gloves from her hands.

Finally, Ifra sat in the chair beside the window and looked at the bodies in her lab, sobbing as tears rolled down her face. After a moment she counted down from ten, stood, and set herself to finding the Baron. This insanity had to end.

15.

Octavius pushed his way through the dining room in a desperate search for the young Leona. Patch and Valentino were grown men and while he hoped he'd find them, he also thought that between them and this little girl, they were the ones that could find their own way out of this mess. The young Balteshezzar, though, was a child and vulnerable to the insane will that had overcome this crowd.

He pushed aside a lovemaking couple, dodged the blasts of a revolver duel, and ducked as a wine glass flew over his head and knocked off his top hat. He kept moving through the chaos, his eyes and ears searching the room for any sign of the little girl. He eventually had made it to the back of the dining room and spied something.

There! He thought, as he saw what appeared to be Leona's dark brown hair running into an eastward corridor. He ran, pushing and shoving until he turned the corner and saw no sign of Leona, but instead a cloaked dwarf rushing through the hall frantically trying to open doors.

"You there! You haven't seen a young girl run through this corridor have you?" Bimblewald called to the figure.

The dwarf ran toward Octavius in a dead sprint, catching the old carnie in big burly hands as he turned to run away, yanking him to the ground with surprising strength. "Where's the Baron?" The dwarf growled, pulling Bimblewald's face to touch his wide nose.

"I haven't the foggiest, sir! Last I saw, he went into the second floor with the Grand Lion. No one's seen him since."

"We've gotta find 'im! You seem to have your wits about ya. Got a clue how to get up to the second floor from here?"

"Begging your pardon, but I've never set foot in this estate before tonight. The only way I know is the stairs in the foyer, and they're guarded by the Rosary Brothers, who don't seem keen on letting anyone pass. Not to mention the several hundred raving lunatics between!"

"Bah! There's always another way, there has to be!" The dwarf kept trying the doors until he pried open a portal to a stairwell. "Ha! A servant's stairway!" he exclaimed then turned to Bimblewald and pointed a stern finger at him. "Listen, 'Mustaches,'" he started, "I'm going to go find the Baron or his goddamned wife, pry the key to the gates outside from them even if it means killin', and get my happy ass as far from this shitshow as my legs can carry me. You can come or not, I don't quite give a shit, but whatever you're doin', you'd best be doin' it right quick-like."

"I'm quite keen on getting out of here myself, sir dwarf, but there's an innocent child somewhere in this estate and I couldn't live with myself if she dies at the hands of one of these maniacs."

"I ain't helpin' ya look for no kid in this mess, 'Mustaches.' You comin' or not?"

Octavius thought for a second. If Leona went anywhere, she might have gone upstairs, perhaps to find her father. "Alright, I'm coming." He said, following the dwarf up the stairs. "My name's Bimblewald, by the way: Octavius Bimblewald."

"Oh yeah? The carnival master? You look a little different than I thought."

"What exactly did you think I would look like?"

"Well, fatter for one."

"Whatever would make you think I'd be fat?"

"Bah! Enough. No time for small talk. My name's Donard. If you call me anything, that'll do."

"A pleasure." Octavius said as they reached the second floor landing.

"We'll work our way up looking for 'im." Donard said, throwing the door open and charging into the corridor.

Bimblewald followed. At the end of the hallway, the two of them ducked as Donard peaked around a corner. "Damn, the clerics are roamin' the halls. We can't tangle with those bastards."

Behind them, they heard the sound of someone clearing their throat. They turned and saw a woman dressed in the tailored ornate garb of the estate staff with a long rip in the hem of her dress. Blood covered her hands and torso.

Donard got between Bimblewald and the newcomer, raising his fists to fight but instead was greeted by a sign of surrender. "I mean you no harm so long as you have your wits about you." She said with a foreign accent.

"We do." Bimblewald responded, putting his arm in front of Donard who gave him a look of incredulity. "Who might you be?"

"My name is Ifra. I am the baron's family doctor."

Donard humphed, "Doin' a piss poor job of it, aren't ya?"

A look of... well Bimblewald couldn't quite tell if it was rage or despair that crossed the doctor's face but either way, she glared at Donard with a passion. "I am a physician, not a one-woman triage, dwarf. I was already ill-stocked for even minor inconveniences, let alone a full-scale break-out of violent lunacy. Whatever is going on here, it is well beyond my expertise."

"Right well, in any case, since you're staff and all, might'nt ya get us past these goons?" Donard flicked his finger toward the hallway where a cleric was marching toward them as they spoke.

"What exactly is your business here anyways?" Ifra asked suspiciously.

Donard began to spit out what Bimblewald guessed would have been a stream of curses before he stopped him. "We are looking for the Baron to help make sense of all this."

"Then we are of the same mind. Follow me closely if you please." Ifra led the way through the corridor.

They walked past the Rosary Brothers, who glared at them from behind their cowls as they passed. Donard looked down at his feet, where each step left a faint print of blood upon the bright red and gold floral carpet. His face turned red and he whispered, "Might'nt we walk a bit more briskly, woman?"

"It's doctor, and not in the name of discretion, dwarf."

"Discretion?" Donard grumbled sarcastically.

Bimblewald kicked Donard on the back of his foot to silence him. They rounded the corner and walked down an eastward hall. Ifra felt the same instinctual dread, smelled the same scent as the Vicar's breath, the closer they moved to the door at the end of the hallway: the one with a plaque beside it reading, "Baron's Office."

Bimblewald was tense, like his senses were the overtense strings of a harp being plucked out of tune and rhythm with the rest of him. His breathing increased and it became harder to keep his heart rate down until finally, the three of them reached the door and Ifra knocked. Donard looked behind them and saw one of the clerics standing back at the last intersection of corridors, still as a statue and glaring right at them. "Uh, woman, what's our friend doing back here?"

Ifra looked back. She was unnerved by the sight as well, by how still the imposing figure stood watching them. "Last I saw, the Grand Lion and the Baron left the festivities. I assumed they went to his office to discuss some business of theirs. Perhaps he is a sign I was right, watching us to make sure we do no harm to their leader." Ifra said this mostly to calm her own thoughts. Nevertheless, she knocked again, this time a bit harder. "My lord, Baron, it's the doctor. We have an emergency that demands your attention."

No answer, but Ifra thought she heard a groan within. "My lord?" Still nothing. She tried the nob and the door opened to a dark room lit only by a candelabra on a large wooden desk. No one sat at the desk, nor was there any sign of the Grand Lion anywhere. Ifra moved cautiously inside until she saw the Baron lying facedown on the rug behind the desk.

As the doctor rushed to his side and began checking his vitals, Donard looked back again and saw the cleric still standing at the intersection, watching them without a single movement. Bimblewald hurried to help Ifra sit the Baron back in his chair, and Donard slowly closed the office door, his eye on the cleric all the way until the door latch clicked.

"He seems to have suffered a seizure of some sort," Ifra said, "but his vitals are fine. My lord?" She tried to wake him.

"Hold on now." Donard whispered. "Don't wake 'im just yet." He dashed toward the desk and began opening drawers and cabinets, then frisking the Baron himself."

"What is the meaning of thi-" Ifra started.

"I'm looking for the bloody key, woman. I have it on good authority that the gates to the estate grounds are locked by a special sort of key that only the Baron's family has."

"It's a magnetic lock, the key is an orb of carefully crafted metal rings that cause the latches to unlock themselves." Ifra said. "The metals of the key and the locking mechanism have an amazing reaction to each other. The system was designed to make looting the estate while the Baron is away almost impossible."

"Almost?" Donard asked.

"Well, a cannon *is* still a cannon, dwarf. At any rate, the Baron, his wife, and the Majordomo all had one of the keys on a necklace." Donard ripped the Baron's shirt open: no necklace. The man himself, however, began to come to.

"Wh…. What? What happened? Where'd that devilish fiend get off to?" The Baron stuttered, struggling to rise from the chair.

"You'd best sit, my lord. Standing is not a good idea right now." Ifra put her hands on the Baron's shoulders and gently pressed him back into the chair.

"That hypocrite. That wicked, monstrous villain cast a curse of some sort on me."

"Who did?" asked Bimblewald.

"The Grand Lion, that's who." The Baron spit.

"What? The Grand Lion using witchery? Absurd."

Donard scoffed, "What Rosary Brother uses magic, eh?" Then, he was reminded of what the native had said before. "Wait a second, I met a native woman who said that a fugitive with skills in Necromancy had escaped the Brotherhood's custody. What if the Lion is an imposter? What if the person they thought was the Grand Lion is this outlaw in disguise.

"Wait, you met an native downstairs?" Bimblewald asked.

"Is that what caught your attention in all that?" Donard asked incredulously.

"If this warlock is indeed posing as the Grand Lion, then the clerics must be told. They will assist us if they know the truth." Said the Baron. "Come! I will have order in my home. Let us hunt down this scum."

The Baron stood with some difficulty and drew a long gun from the corner of the office where it leaned against a wall. He took it, fitted it with a bayonet, and strode toward the office door. When he opened it, just halfway down the hallway stood the dark cleric that had been watching them. "Soldier of the Rosary Brotherhood of Clerics, you have been deceived." He called, marching toward the sentinel with confidence.

Ifra felt her hair stand up along her spine and her eyes dilated. Donard too stood still, causing Bimblewald to pause in confusion. The Baron continued to inform the cleric of the situation until he got close. Then, the great robed gargoyle grabbed the Baron's arm and the three fellows watched as the lord of the house was bashed like a ragdoll into the walls of the hallway. The sounds of bones cracking reached their ears and Donard grabbed the door, throwing it closed.

"Help me!" the dwarf called, grabbing the Baron's desk and flipping it over. Ifra got on the other side of it and the two began pushing it toward the door as a huge archaic mace burst through wood. Bimblewald stumbled back, all his senses spiraling into a vortex of pure terror. His back hit glass and stone as he turned to see the office window overlooking the botanical gardens below. Trapped.

Crash! The cleric broke through the door, Donard and Ifra falling back as the hooded horror booted the desk toward the window. Bimblewald looked paralyzed at the Rosary Brother preparing to swing the mace at *him* this time. Then, the sound of glass breaking and a sinking sensation in his gut interrupted his frozenness. Octavius felt an abrupt thud and saw dust and glass falling all around them. All went black as the old carnie's mind retreated to the only safety it had left. Unconsciousness.

16.

There she was, his beautiful wife. His paramore. The mother of his muse. The most difficult relationship he'd ever had the willingness to cultivate. She wept before him. "You're drinking again?" she cried.

"You have no idea what I'm going through!" Octavius heard himself shout, part of him wondering why he'd ever raised his voice at her. "You think you can come here with a ring on your finger again and expect me to forget all the times you tried to take everything from me? No! You can't, and you won't." He watched her cry for a moment in the solipsistic haze just before waking back up on the warm stone floor of the greenhouse.

"What happened?" he said as his senses slowly returned. The ground around them was covered in shattered glass, which he was very careful not to cut himself on as he rose to his feet.

"No time." Donard said, grabbing him by the arm and pulling him along. Ifra had already risen and gone to the greenhouse external door to check outside for danger. When she'd ascertained that they were clear, the three of them rushed through the botanical gardens away from the estate proper.

"Where are we goin'?" Donard said.

"The barracks for the baron's police detail. With these Rosary Brothers against us, we need to find help and hopefully some of the officers are there." Ifra stated.

The dwarf had reservations but what other option was before them? If they went back to the estate, they'd die. If the guards were duplicitous, they'd die. At least this way, if the guards were even halfway decent, they might get some help. The image of the cleric looming over them, gazing down from the broken office window through the shattered roof of the greenhouse warned him that soon, whatever the case, they'd have every one of those whoresons on top of them.

As they reached the estate's outer wall, the guard barracks came into view. A long wooden two-story building extending along the interior of the wall with a lean-to roof. Bimblewald followed them fighting his mental and emotional exhaustion. He had the growing sensation like he was a piece of clothing being pulled apart at seams, a feeling that at any moment he could simply be unhinged and lose all control over his body. He began to think how much easier it would be to just fall to the ground and sleep.

When they'd at last crossed the great open yard between the gardens and the barracks, their bodies bathed in silver moonlight that exposed them to any eyes spying their way, they reached the door. Donard and Ifra began trying to open it, one hissing, "It's locked!" and the other grumbling, "Out of the way, I'll handle it."

Meanwhile Bimblewald saw to the west the shape of a little girl illuminated by the moon. *Leona!* He thought. He looked over at the others and pointed toward her saying, "The Baron's daughter! She's alive." They looked in the direction he'd indicated and then back at him confused. Bimblewald didn't have the time to argue with them, he had to take the opportunity to catch up to her. The clerics would surely be searching for her, and after seeing what became of her father he simply couldn't let her be hunted like an animal through her own home.

He turned to run toward her when he felt Donard's firm grip yank him back toward the barracks. "Leona!" Octavius cried, and thought he saw her look back at him before the doctor's hand clapped over his mouth.

"What the fuck do ya think you're doin', 'Bimbleballs?'" The dwarf growled. "Saint's fucking cock, you tryin' to give us away?"

"The girl I was looking for is over there. She heard me. We can't just let her die."

72

"Listen friend," Ifra said calmly in his ear, "we didn't see anyone over there. You're in shock, not to mention you may have jogged your head in the fall. Please stay close to us. If we see the girl, we'll help."

Donard grumbled something about Ifra speaking for himself. "It's not just any girl, doctor. It's Leona Balteshezzar!" Octavius said, trying to emphasize the gravity of the situation.

With that, both of them looked wide-eyed at Bimblewald. "Well, then we'll be doubly sure to help." Ifra conceded.

Even Donard agreed. He hadn't the slightest care about the girl's life though as in his mind, the young Leona was worth saving for other reasons. Afterall, he hadn't been able to steal any 'goods' for his fence yet. Perhaps the living daughter of a baron could fetch a fine price for her prospective ransom profits. He'd kept that idea to himself however.

Donard turned back to the door and brandished the tools of his trade. The other two ignored this as it wasn't really the time to pry. Instead they looked out into the gardens, running their eyes over every inch in search of pursuers.

With a click, the barracks door creaked ajar and all three of them made their way in quickly, Donard closing the door behind them. Their noses were immediately greeted with the pungent stench of gallons of blood in puddles at their feet. Bimblewald gasped and stumbled back as his foot knocked against a limp hand. There in the middle of the floor was a mound of bloody corpses, each one in a police uniform.

The three of them were stunned. It had to be the entire detail. Donard looked all around the room, under every bunk and in every footlocker. Not a single weapon was left. "Come on," the dwarf said, covering his nose,

73

"let's check the second level. At the very least, we might find somethin' useful."

They followed him as he stepped carefully over the bodies. They went through a door that opened into the interior of the walls, looked right and saw a hatch door. "What's that?" Donard asked.

"Tunnels beneath the estate." Ifra answered, "There are hatches that connect to the kitchen, barracks, and wine cellar. I've never seen them, but I've heard the servants speak of a chamber full of pipes and valves that allow engineers to control the plumbing."

"That could come in handy." Donard stated.

The three of them turned left and ascended a stairwell to the second level of the barracks. This bay was empty save for the furnishing. The only difference was a small office at the other end of the building. "That's the office of the detail's captain." Ifra said.

"Is that right? Well then you two spread out and search for anything useful. I'll go pick the lock to the office." Donard said hurrying across the bay.

He didn't have to work very hard before he pushed the door open and saw the decapitated body of someone who he could only guess was the captain. He entered and searched the captain's body, finding that his baton was gone, but there was a piece of the desk that struck the blacksmith as odd. He felt around the underside of the desk and soon his hand ran over a thin partition in the otherwise smooth piece of carpentry.

He felt around the area and sensed the cuts forming a rectangle, with a small square of cuts in one of its corners. Curious, he pushed against the rectangle, feeling the wood lift a little bit. Then, he pressed his finger into the square and felt the greater shape fall open at an angle. Inside this secret compartment was a small pistol, not quite big enough to be standard issue equipment but definitely small enough to hide for dire circumstances. He took the weapon, along with a full magazine that was also in the compartment, and continued his examination of the desk.

He looked through papers and ledgers. He unfolded one piece of parchment to reveal what looked like a blueprint of sorts. "Ifra!" he called in a loud whisper. The doctor made her way to the office, where Donard showed her the image. "Is this somewhere in the estate?"

"No, I've never seen or heard of this." Ifra responded.

Donard looked around the room and saw maps of the various levels of the palace framed on the wall. He began examining the prints while Octavius stumbled his way into the office. The darkness was oppressive to him. He looked around and saw only slivers of pale, cold moonlight streaming in through small slits above the bunks. He'd begun to hear wicked sounds emanating all around him, like screams muffled by the darkness, whirling in the elemental shadows themselves like a strong wind upon the walls outside.

"What the fuck?" Donard said.

"What is it?" Ifra inquired, prompting the dwarf to hold the parchment against a map of the lowest level. There was a discrepancy in the map, a section that by all appearances should have a chamber but didn't. The parchment Donard held detailed a lower level in this missing section where a large rotunda seemed to connect to a subterranean waterway deep beneath the estate.

Just then, they all heard the door to the barracks below burst open and the sound of heavy boots marching slowly through the bay below toward the staircase.

17.

"Hide!" Donard hissed. Bimblewald ducked under the captain's desk, Donard hurried to an armoire and entered, closing the doors behind him. Ifra crawled under a bunk, holding her mouth shut to silence any involuntary intonations of fear.

The sound of each footstep thumping up the stairs sent the companions' hearts racing. When the cleric reached the door to the upper bay, it swung open and the dark visage of the robes burst through the door. This one was carrying a kite shield concealing his body save for his shoulders and head, and in his other hand carried an antique sword with strange symbols engraved into the hilt. Ifra felt her eyes narrow, her heart thumping like a drum in her chest, filling every inch of her with adrenaline. Everything in her screamed to be still, to be silent.

The heavy footsteps were the only discernible sound emanating from the wraith's existence. He didn't even seem to be breathing or at least if he was he was doing so extremely quietly. Bimblewald heard the footsteps stop halfway through the bay. He looked underneath the desk's backboard and saw the cleric standing stock still, looking directly at the bunk Ifra was under. *No!* He screamed in his head, but he couldn't bring himself to do anything for the doctor. He just watched as the cleric walked over to the bed, lifted his broadsword for a stab…

Then, the room erupted with commotion! Ifra rolled out from under the bed and rushed on all between the bunks dodging sword slashes. Donard burst from the armoire and a thunderous crack split their eardrums. The cleric stopped swinging at Ifra and swung about to face Donard, who hollered, "Pimplefled, go on!" Octavius ran behind the dwarf as he cracked off another shot that obviously hit the cleric but caused very little pause before the horrible figure began rushing toward them with his shield out in front like a wall barrelling toward them. Bimblewald dove through a bunk, landed on the next one down and rolled off it, sprinting toward the door.

Donard waited until the cleric was on him, then dogged left to avoid getting hit by the fiend's shield. Then, the dwarf hopped up on the nearest bunk and followed suit with Bimblewald, narrowly avoiding a decapitating swing of the cleric's sword as the horror wheeled about to give them chase.

The three rushed down the stairwell and Ifra ran to the hatch, threw it open and started climbing down the ladder, Donard and Bimblewald close behind. Octavius started descending the ladder just as the sound of running boots began thudding down the stairs. He closed the hatch behind them and quickly descended. Below, he heard the other two running in the darkness that had completely blinded him. He ran after the sounds of their footsteps, feeling for the walls as he did.

It seemed to him that the tunnels were cylindrical and walled with stone bricks. The darkness was crushing, even more so as he heard the echoes of the others' footsteps sounding him. Sometimes he felt he was running beside them, but when he reached out, no one was there.

The echoes grew louder and louder, not as if growing closer but more like their sound was bearing down on him. He felt confused and lost as he turned in the darkness. Where was he? Had he made a wrong turn somewhere? Where were the others? Could they hear his steps too? If so, why had they abandoned him? Or did he abandon them somewhere along the way?

The images of Patch and Valentino appeared to him. The thought that they'd been brutally murdered somewhere in the estate crushed him. He'd left them to their fate. He'd given up on his search for them. All to try to find the young Leona instead. She didn't even know him! Why would he abandon his colleagues, his friends, to search for this girl?

What did she look like again? Brown eyes? No, blue. Blue eyes, like his wife! And auburn hair, or was it Blonde? Octavius' thoughts muddled the more he thought. Where were Patch and Valentino anyways? He should have at least spotted them through the crowds. He knew where they were performing: the Foyer! The Foyer where all the blood had been spilled. Blood!

Something wet dripped on his head. "For fuck's sake stop running!" He heard the vulgar dwarf say, or was it him who shouted that. He wanted the echoes to stop. It was impossible to think with all the racket. He looked around and everything was completely dark! Where was he? The tunnels felt cylindrical and possibly made of stone bricks, he thought. The sheer emptiness of these tunnels was blasphemous. It was like light was a lie he'd been told. That this darkness was more real than his memories of illumination.

What? He heard voices! No words though. Just consonants on the edges of his senses, like trying to listen to a conversation spoken in whispers from across a room. They were all around him though. Was he in some sort of chamber? He walked in all directions feeling for the walls. They weren't there! There were no walls!

The floor started to feel like it was moving beneath his feet. The old carnie wretched and threw up wine and hors d'oeuvres as a sudden feeling of vertigo assaulted him and fell to the ground. Rolling onto his back, he lifted his hands to his face. Even with his palm on his nose, he couldn't see it.

Again something wet dripped on him, then again and again. He felt thirsty from vomiting and opened his mouth. As soon as he tasted the substances he wretched again: the mingled flavor of blood and mead. Then, the slow drips fell more and more, until it was like rain drenching his face and coat.

His body and voice spasmed in panic. He tried to get to his feet, slipping once or twice. Then, he heard a voice through the downpour. He tried to wipe his eyes of the viscous, sticky liquid as he ran in circles, desperate to find a door or even a wall to guide himself by. The voice grew louder, until he finally knew it. "Valentino, old chap! Heavens, are you okay?" he shouted moving toward the voice.

"No, Octavius. I'm not." Valentino's young voice said shakily.

The voice grew closer and the deluge began to stop. "What happened, my boy? Are you hurt?"

Valentino's voice screamed as if weeping, "I am nothing, Mr. Bimblewald. I'm a charlatan, a false god leading the masses astray. I sell snake oils to the people."

"What are you going on about Valentino? Come now, have you a light?"

"No! You pitiless old fool, no." The boyish voice dropped back into whining. "I'm fake! My life is devoted to illusions of illusions, to slight-of-hand and parlor tricks. I am a blasphemer, Octavius! A godless hack! These shadows bring truth, Octavius. You can hear it? Yes! Listen to it. It'll touch you, tell you things you'll wish you'd never known. The secrets of the innermost."

"By heavens, what do you speak of, Valentino? Quit with the poetics, I'm not one of your strumpets!"

"I...is...is this your card, Mr. Bimblewald? Please tell me. Tell me I'm extraordinary. Tell me that I'm... I'm special." More weeping.

"I can't see the card, Valentino, and I never picked one. Now come on." Bimblewald was sure he was right in front of the boy, judging by his voice. He reached out to grab him and felt nothing.

"He made me disappear, Octavius." The voice said. "It wasn't a trick! I ran from the foyer, down the servant's stairs, into the tunnels. One of the Rosary Brothers grabbed me and bagged my head, took me through the tunnels to some big chamber and... I saw him. No! Don't ask me to explain who he is, what he is! Please Octavius. It hurts my tongue to describe it. All I know is that he... he knew! And... and I knew it, and ... and ... he knew that I knew it when I knew it. Then," he began to laugh maniacally in between snotty sniffles, "A magician never shares his secrets."

Bimblewald reached again, knowing, absolutely knowing that he was right in front of the boy. But there was nothing. All that his senses detected was the void where poor Valentino *should* be. The voice stopped and Bimblewald heard the sounds of heavy footsteps thudding through the tunnel beside him, then he was jerked back and dragged away from Valentino in tears.

18.

The darkness in the tunnels was impenetrable. Ifra waited a moment to hear Donard and Bimblewald's footsteps behind her before starting to run again. She limited her speed to a light jog in order to avoid tripping or losing track of which direction they were going. She thought that perhaps if she kept her wits about her, she might be able to guide them to the wine cellar hatch. She mustered all the hope she had left to believe that the wine cellar would be empty.

Just then, she felt one of her companions rush past her in the darkness. "Heavens! Have they caught up to us?" She looked back, sensing that only one had passed.

"Not that I can hear, but 'Gimblewelp' just took off." She heard Donard say.

"Shit! He'll get lost for certain. Did he say anything?"

"Yeah, he was talkin' nonsense, whisperin' to himself somethin' about a girl named Esmerelda's hair color being the same as his wife's, and then about lookin' for folks named Patch and Valen-somthin'. Just about ran over me when he took off."

"We'll have to follow his footsteps. I'll try to keep track of where we are." With that, Ifra and Donard began to pursue Bimblewald through the tunnels calling after him, first in whispers then in contained shouts.

For a moment they'd nearly caught up with him, prompting Donard to yell, "For fuck's sake, stop running!"

But he was gone again, and Ifra heard Donard stop moving. "Come now, we can't let him get too far."

"If you're that keen on gettin' lost in these tunnels, be my guest, but I'm following my own good senses out of this darkness. I couldn't care less if he's lost his."

"If he was mumbling about finding someone, perhaps helping him would give him more focus." Ifra said pleadingly. The idea of braving this darkness alone was terrifying, not to mention the notion of trying to escape the grounds by herself if they were... eternally separated.

"Sure, I heard him. He's been buggin' me about 'findng people' since we met, but I'll not be stickin' my neck out that far tonight. The Osterian Duke's ransom for the girl wouldn't be enough to go the way the old baron did, rest his bastard soul."

"Ransom? What are you talking about ransom?" Ifra asked.

Donard cleared his throat a bit, cursing himself inwardly, "I... it's, uh, well it's just an expression. I'm just sayin' I don't intend on dyin' for some little girl, Baron's daughter or no."

Kitraan's eyes narrowed. "What were you doing in the estate tonight anyways? You're no noble, I've seen how *they* dress themselves. Not one of them would leave their homes looking like you."

"I told you, I was at the festival when a native found me and told me that the only way off the grounds was to find the Baron's key, so I ran inside to find the cocky fuck. What's any of that got to do with our gettin' out of the these tunnels? Let's get moving."

Just then the two of them heard those terrible trudging footsteps echoing through the halls behind and in front of them. *Fuck! Took too long,* the dwarf thought, *should have just ditched this bitch instead of meanderin' around!* He and Ifra quickly turned down the passage that Bimblewald had run down.

Careful to control the volume of their steps, the two hurried down the passage. They walked step by step, ears pricked for the sounds of the clerics. Eventually they began to hear a voice in the distance. Their pace quickened until they entered a more open room. Ifra couldn't see anything but she heard Bimblewald ahead of them in the darkness. She heard the carnie ask, "Who did you see?"

"Dwarf, he's over here." Ifra hissed. Both of them followed the sound of Bimblewald's voice.

Bimblewald didn't seem to have noticed them, apparently listening to something they couldn't hear. Ifra's heart skipped a beat at the sound of the clerics' footsteps in the hallway just outside the room. "Dwarf, they're in the tunnels! We have to move."

Once they were close enough to the voice that he could tell the old carnie was just in front of him, Donard grabbed Bimblewald by his waistcoat and tried pulling him back. He almost screamed before Ifra wrapped her hand around his mouth, whispering in his ear, "Octavius, be quiet! The clerics are almost on us."Once they had the old man under control, Donard found the edge of the room and located a new hallway, calling the others to join him.

They walked a short ways, before Bimblewald finally spoke. "Where did the two of you go? I tried searching for you but I must have gotten lost."

"'Searchin' for us?' You ran from us. We had to go lookin' for you!" Donard said indignantly.

"He's right." Ifra concurred. "You nearly ran into me as you passed us."

"What?" Octavius began to feel sick with confusion. "Am I going mad?"

"You're stressed, Mr. Bimblewald. The night has been a traumatic one for all of us." Ifra's voice was intentionally reassuring, and she gently put her hand on his shoulder to comfort him. She knew they couldn't continue on while he was suffering whatever psychosis was affecting him, but there was nothing to be done at this moment other than console him until they found somewhere relatively safe.

"Or," Donard's voice rose grimly, "the Grand Lion is casting a spell on him as we speak."

"Would you be quiet, Mister…" Ifra stopped when she realized he hadn't actually shared his last name with her during their introductions.

"Jünghoeffer" Donard said.

"I'll just stick with Donard, then."

"What if he's right, doctor?" Bimblewald asked. "What if I'm under the same spell that drove everyone else mad?"

"I'm not convinced there is any magic at play here." Ifra responded. "More likely, the Grand Lion poisoned the wine with some sort of mind-affecting toxin."

"Didn't you drink the wine as well?"

"I did."

"And you haven't suffered any ill effects?"

"Not yet. It's possible I didn't drink enough for it to affect me, or it's affecting me more slowly than it has others."

"What about you, Donard? Didn't you drink any wine."

"Not a drop." The blacksmith answered flatly.

"Alright so, it could have been a poison. But why? Why would the Grand Lion attack us? The baron was a supporter of the Rosary Brothers."

"I cannot answer that." Ifra said. "Perhaps to incite war with the natives of this country? Why else would one of them be here trying to stop it?"

"If that were so," Donard started, "why wouldn't the native I met have told me as such? She seemed pretty convinced that the Grand Lion was a witch of some sort."

"Cultural misunderstanding, maybe? Perhaps the natives consider the toxin that the Grand Lion used to be magical?"

"Or maybe they know more than we do about this disaster." Donard said curtly.

A moment of silence passed before they entered another large room. "I think we're below the kitchen now, if I remember correctly." Ifra said.

They all began searching the room, finding the walls first and running their hands along them for a door. They found nothing, and all was silent before the unmistakable sound of the clerics' boots could be heard in the hallway they'd come from. "There's no other hallway to go through!" Donard called to the others.

They all began to feel panic setting in, but with her last clear thought, Ifra ran to the center of the room. *A ladder!* "There's a ladder here, come on!" She heard the other's footsteps hurry toward her just as the clerics' picked up speed. All three of them climbed the ladder and at the top, found a locked hatch. "Damn it!" Ifra gasped.

She felt the ladder shudder a bit, then Donard's voice in front of her said, "Climb down!"

Below them, the clerics could be heard entering the room. "They're here!" Octavius cried.

Ifra heard Donard begin to bang on the hatch above just as Bimblewald began kicking at the clerics attempting to climb up after them. The sound of a thud and a crash from a pursuer falling to the ground below. "Hurry!" Ifra cried frantically.

Donard let out a furious roar and beat one last time on the hatch, which busted open at the hinge. Moonlight flashed into the room as he threw open the door and climbed up. The others followed with the clerics just below them on the ladder.Up in the kitchen, Doanrd searched the room for weapons, eventually finding a large paring knife and butcher's blade. He rushed back to the hatch where the others had just climbed up, pulled out the pistol and fired a shot into the face of the first cleric he saw climbing up after them.

The body dropped down and knocked the second pursuer off the ladder. Then, Donard took the butcher's blade and hacked into the ladder. As both the clerics got back up and began to climb, the cuts he'd made on both sides of the ladder gave way. Both clerics fell back to the chamber's floor and Donard shut the hatch. "They'll have to find another way through the tunnels." Donard said, breathing heavily. opened it and they ran in. It was a stairwell leading up.

They slowly recovered their senses. None of them felt quite comfortable about being back in the estate, but at this point, there was nowhere they could go that'd be safe from the Rosary Brothers hunting them. At least for the moment, though, things seemed quiet. The silvery moonlight filtered into the room through narrow windows at the tops of the walls.

Ifra listened in every direction for the movement of thundering footsteps while Donard checked how much ammunition the dead captain's pistol had left and eyed the maps he'd swiped from the office. Bimblewald sat beside a cupboard, rubbing his temples with a confused look on his face. All each of them could think of was how desperately they wanted to be rid of the place.

19.

Octavius' skin was clammy and pale, revealing the deep shadows of his rough hands, which were trembling violently. He reached into his waist coat for his flask. Nothing in the left side pocket, he reached for the right. Nothing there either. It was gone! His flask was gone. He'd dropped it somewhere along the way. He stood up quickly and immediately fell back on his haunches as his head split and he saw lights floating around him. The moonlight glared and hurt his eyes.

Ifra noticed this and hurried over to him. "Stay seated, Mr. Bimblewald." She said, placing two fingers to the carnie's left wrist. The man's pulse was rapid. Ifra observed Bimblewald's staggering breaths. "I need you to take deep breaths now, Octavius."

Bimblewald tried to comply as he watched the doctor look around the dark kitchen. He closed his eyes for a moment to keep out the silver light, and soon felt a leathery hand slapping him gently. "Don't sleep! Stay awake." he heard the doctor's voice say. He felt a rather heavy mound of aprons and towels get thrown over him. They were warm, or rather he just hadn't realized how cold he felt.

"Keep breathing, sir."

"What's wrong with him?" He heard Donard say.

"He's definitely in shock, but something else is happening to him as well. He seems to be exhibiting signs of a…" Ifra paused

"A what?"

"Do tell, doctor." Octavius heard his own shaky voice say.

Ifra bent down and looked the old carnie in the eyes, "Mr. Bimblewald, have you any history with hallucinations?"

Bimblewald looked at her confused. "No, doctor. Bad dreams and a bit of hard liquor, but I've never had hallucinations. Before you say another word, I'll tell you now that I was not hallucinating down there." He pushed the blankets off and slowly stood up. *I wasn't hearing things,* he thought to himself. *Was I?*

He began walking slowly around the room, making sure to focus on something as he went. It seemed to help keep the nausea away as the room blurred around him. He reached for the cabinets and drawers, opening them quietly to look for anything fermented he might be able to drink.

Ifra heard something then, something in the room with them. She followed the sound. Donard noticed the doctor's silent movements and was about to ask if she'd heard something before she shushed him. Bimblewald watched the doctor nervously. Ifra reached a pantry on the far side of the room, and knocked silently on the door.

From within they heard a yelp. The doctor opened the door to reveal one of the palace chefs. "Ho! Oh! Nay, madmen! Nay!" the cook yelled in a high pitched voice. Donard looked infuriatingly at him and Ifra clapped a hand over the man's mouth.

"Silence, fool! You want to bring the Clerics down on us?" Donard whispered excitedly.

The chef pulled Ifra's hand away from his mouth. "The Clerics? Heavens, am I to believe the Rosary Brothers are trying to kill us as well?"

"What d'ya mean 'as well,' cook?" Donard asked.

"I'm a chef, dwarf, and I mean to say that there are maniacs about, attacking anyone they see. The Clerics disappeared on us not long after everyone went stark raving mad. You're the doctor around here aren't you? Have any idea what's going on?"

"No, I haven't." Ifra answered, "I went to the Baron, and he seemed to think it was magic, but then he was killed by one of the clerics."

"Killed? By a fucking Roseman? And Magic?" The chef's voice increased in pitch and he was about to howl before Ifra silenced him again. He fainted for a moment before the doctor slapped him a few times.

"Huh? What? Did I faint? Yes? By heavens, I don't have the constitution for this lunacy."

Donard walked up to the man and shoved the small map depicting the missing room in his face. "Got a clue where this is?" He asked.

"Not in the slightest. Is that here in the palace?"

Donard grumbled as he walked away from the chef.

Ifra looked the man in the eye, speaking calmly, "Listen. We have to get out of here. Have you seen the Majordomo or the Chamberlain?"

"Uh, no. Well least ways not the majordee. The chamberlain came down and asked if we'd seen the wine tampered with in any way, which I hadn't. He went down to the cellar there," he gestured to an open door with a shallow staircase, "to check it for himself."

Ifra looked into the darkness, wondering if she was right and the wine *had* been poisoned after all. Perhaps that was why the Clerics killed the Baron and were attacking them. If the wine had been poisoned by the Grand Lion, then the Clerics might be hunting anyone unaffected by the toxin. However, she was out of her depth in such matters, and hadn't a single idea how to be certain, which disconcerted her greatly.

Could she go mad then? She had drunk the wine and no matter how small the amount, she was well aware of the level to which one's mortal senses might deceive them under the influence of certain substances. The body was a fickle, frail mechanism afterall, and the mind is easily coerced. Then, she looked at Bimblewald. The man was obviously in distress. Something in the tunnels had obviously addled him, or maybe his mind was just starting to feel the effects of the toxin.

She wondered what this meant for her, feeling her heart begin to race, imagining herself going mad and murdering people as she'd seen the guests doing. She shook the thought from her mind as best she could and called Bimblewald over to her.

The carnie rose to his feet and approached. "Yes, good doctor?"

Ifra reached into the bag at her side and pulled out a little vial of light anesthetic. "Will you take this? It'll help calm your nerves."

"Right. Thank you, doctor." Before Bimblewald could take the small vessel, they all heard a voice emanate from the small staircase that led up into the dining room.

"Missing something, Octavius?" Bimblewald looked and saw the silhouette of a jester's hat, only half of a smiling mask showing in the light from the windows, held with one hand against the figure's face. In the other was a top hat and a flask.

20.

"Patch?" Bimblewald looked around to make sure everyone else was seeing the jester sitting on the staircase. It would seem that they were as the chef whined dramatically and grabbed a cast iron pan off of a stove top, holding it shakily toward the clown. "Patch, my good man. What fortune! I thought you might be dead."

Patch stood, holding his mirthly mask up to his face with one hand and replacing the hat and flask with his weeping mask in the other. His old pitchy voice began to rattle on in rhyme:

"Hours of mirthless midnight I have ambled,
And finally before me
Is the Lieutenant of Troubadours,
the Commander Carnie.
'Where did he go,'
I wondered as I wandered?
'Perhaps down below'
So down I went, I shall not lie
When a maniacal magician found I.
'Pick a card,' said he
and I did to see
The Jack of Hearts I do decree.
Such fun, I thought, was this game we were playing,
That a knife I drew
to start at the flaying!
But woe had I when I began at my grind,
To see that no heart
in this man did I find!
A ghost was he, deprived of his body…"

Patch stumbled in his meter, let out a growl of frustration and switched the mask to the sorrowful sort. "Body… Body… what rhymes, what rhymes?" The jesters frustration built and the party looked at each other, begging each other to do something.

"Uh, toddy, snotty, naughty…" Bimblewald began rattling off rhymes, gesturing for the others to begin moving toward the cellar door.

"Yes!" the clown exclaimed and finished the verse:

"Taken from him by a wizard, quite naughty!"

The clown had been walking closer and closer to Bimblewald, who himself had been backing away toward the cellar door. Donard decided to circle around the lyricist and go up into the dining room. He gestured for Ifra to follow him and the two slowly inched along the kitchen perimeter until they reached the stairs. Bimblewald and the chef had continued backward, but they'd backed into a corner and Patch was within arm's reach.

"Patch, my good man. Are you speaking of Valentino? Are you saying he's…"

"Quite dead, aye, the magician is.
And he was right deserving.
You remember protecting his bliss,
his sexual unnerving.
He was broken young lad
From the very start!
Yet, even as he was bad,
You guarded his gambling art."

Bimblewald looked down. Many of his carnies had troubled pasts, and even after joining the Circus, they'd often continued in some criminal behaviors. Octavius remembered many a time when, upon Valentino's return from town, he'd had to pay recompense to men for the… defilement of their daughters or for the abuse of their betting games. "Patch, Valentino was troubled, I was only…"

"No more troubled than thee,
Master charlatan!
Remember how became you free
Wife partisan!
Drink had you,

A bit to much
And your anger flew
To violence and such."
Bimblewald shook his head as thoughts of his wife flashed before him. "Stop it, Patch. I ... don't know what you're talking about." *I loved my wife,* Octavius thought to himself, *I'd never do such a thing to her!*

Just then, Donard took a step up the stairs. The wooden plank beneath his foot creaked. Patch twirled about, switching the mask to the woeful one and saying:
"Where are you going?
You'll miss the show!
Try to leave and I'll get low
You dirty fucking dwarf! I'll cut your eyes out!"

Patch's verse diverged into a wrathful string of obscenities so vile it should never be repeated. His aging joints popped as he rushed at Donard and Ifra. Bimblewald grabbed a bottle of wine from the counter behind him, dashed forward and smashed it over the clown's head. "Stop this wickedness, Patch. Please, I beg of you." Octavius said, his emotions building inside like an impending eruption. He couldn't bear the guilt rising within. Guilt for leaving Patch and Valentino to their fates, for losing the little girl in the chaos, and for... everything else. All the things that he'd hidden in the recesses of his mind, the things that Patch's words had drawn from the deepest darkness.

Patch cried furiously and held his head. The glass bottle had smacked his old cranium with such splitting force that a line of blood was rolling down his neck from beneath his jester's cap. After a moment, the clown began laughing hysterically and turned toward Bimblewald, holding up the merry mask and dropping the mirthless one to the ground. "Please, Patch. Come to your senses, old chap." Bimblewald pleaded.

The laughing drowned out the carnival master's words. Patch drew a butcher's blade from the counter and brandished it menacingly toward Octavius. "It's too late, old friend. The voices in the darkness have called for blood sport and they shall have it!"

Bimblewald dodged to the side to avoid a slash, fast enough to avoid impalement but not enough to avoid getting a flesh wound along his side. Patch swung a backlash. Octavius threw his hands up to stop the knife, but was too early and the blade gashed both his palms. Bimblewald fell back on his knees and cried in pain. The chef squealed and ran for the cellar.

"No, little piggy! We shan't have that!" Patch cried and attacked the chef, goring the back of his head and neck with the blade and then throwing him into the corner of the kitchen. Patch stood over him and cut his throat so that his screams of terror resembled pig squeals, then slashed again and again.

Donard darted up the stairs into the dining room. Ifra looked at Bimblewald holding his hands, and Patch butchering the chef. She couldn't bring herself to leave the old carnie behind so, drawing a scalpel from her bag, she sped silently behind the murderous jester and, with one swift stroke, jabbed the scalpel just at the base of the old man's skull. It was a perfect strike. The clown fell backward into a fit of violent convulsions for several long minutes until he finally stopped moving.

Ifra turned toward the chef, who despite being butchered beyond recognition, still gurgled his own blood. The doctor knew there was nothing to do for him and turned away, hurrying instead to Bimblewald's side. The carnival master sobbed weakly, his hands covered in blood.

The doctor searched the room and found a drawer of hand towels. She gathered them and took them to Octavius, holding his hands and wrapping them tightly.

"Take this now." She handed Bimblewald the anesthetic, and the man drank it eagerly.

21.

Donard bolted up the stairs as the commotion began in the kitchen. He wasn't going to stick around while that clown killed all of them. However, the dining room seemed no more concerting than the kitchen. At the top of the stairs, all Donard could smell was blood and mead. The floor was littered with corpses, bottles, and scraps of mangled food items.

He carefully stepped his way over the bodies and up the great table covered in broken bones of roast beasts. All over the table was gore, wine, and a mess of savaged luxuries. He looked about, listened for something, anything. It was in vain. He came to the realization that everyone at the party had died. Not only that, but by their positions, they'd been killed. Killed by each other.

He even recognized a body amongst them, or rather a badge. It was the badge of the Smithing Union messenger that had visited him that morning. Donard hopped down from the table and began to rummage about the man's remains. He took the badge and guild signet ring, then reached into the man's coat, pulling out a small pouch of coins and a letter. A letter addressed to Donard Jünghoeffer.

The dwarf grabbed a knife off the table and cleaned the grease and blood off of it with his shirt. Cutting through the envelope, he pulled out a folded paper that read:

"Dear Master Jünghoeffer,

It is with great pleasure that the Smith and Metallurgists' Union of the Greater Northwest Frontier informs the recipient of his promotion to the position of Master in the art of Blacksmithing within the guild. This rank is also accredited by the Craftsmen's Guild of the Shevic Basin and the Union of Osterian Smiths and Foundrymen. With this rank, you are permitted by your chosen union of membership to build an establishment within their jurisdiction and engage in the training of apprentices..."

The rest of the letter was instructions on the proper channels of receiving discounted materials for educational purposes and so on, but Donard didn't go through all that. For a moment he just read over that paragraph again. He'd taken in with this clandestine group of sneak-thieves just to earn enough money to get out of Verdendale, but here was a letter from his day job informing him that he could go almost anywhere he wished. If he had only opened the damn door this morning, he might not have even been in this estate tonight.

Then, in front of him, he saw something move. It was small and fast, leaving Donard unsure if it wasn't just a trick of the eyes. The doubts fled when he saw it again. A corpse buried beneath a pile of gore and death was lifting a hand and grabbing at the other bodies, clawing its way out from underneath the other dead. Donard scurried back to the stairs and slid down them silently.

Below he saw Bimblewald drink something from a bottle the doctor had given him. "*Pst!*" They looked at him confused. "Time to go, you two. Somethin's happenin' up there and I ain't keen to stick around for it." He snuck past them towards the cellar door.

"What now?" Ifra asked, walking towards the stairs. Donard tried to tell him to stop, but he'd already reached the base and looking up, saw in the moonlight the pale face of a dead man crawling toward him. The corpse's teeth were gnashing and its arms reached for Ifra hungrily.

The doctor shrieked involuntarily and hurried over to Donard, helping Bimblewald up on the way. "What's happening?" The old carnie asked just before the cold corpse rolled down the stairs. Octavius started and looked back at it, all the blood draining from his face as the gnashing, gurgling mouth rose from the ground. The eyes stared at him with a blasphemous green glow and a look of horrid intent. The clothes hung tattered over the man's body. Then, it slowly began moving its cracking joints toward him.

Ifra pulled Bimblewald back and they all ran to the cellar, descending the stairs, dashing through the door at the bottom and closing it behind them. "Merciful heavens, was that man alive?" Bimblewald asked desperately of his comrades.

"No way. You see how torn up he was? Nothin' could live with wounds like that." Donard said with just an ever so slight hint of panic in his voice.

"It is possible that-" Ifra began.

"He was dead, I tell you! Dead! Stone cold, every last one of them in that dinin' room was dead as a doornail doctor, and don't go tryin' to tell me otherwise!" Ifra went silent. "We're dealin' with a bona fide necromancer!"

"What would a necromancer want in Verdendale?" Bimblewald asked.

"Us." replied the doctor, allowing herself for just a moment to accept the possibility. "I am no expert on paranormal matters, but I read a book today describing to a detail everything we've experienced tonight. People engaging in murderous riots or acts of debauchery, the dead rising, even..." Ifra looked at Bimblewald, "...hallucinations. If the Grand Lion is a necromancer, then he is gaining power every second from the souls that died on these grounds."

"Well he ain't havin' mine." Donard exclaimed, leaving the light emanating from the slit under the doorway and going into the darkness in search of a way out. "Ain't nothing stealin' my soul though, nor yours." He trapsed around the dark cellar for a moment before he saw something in the far end.

"Perhaps... Perhaps the Grand Lion *did* poison the wine, specifically the Honeysuckle Mead, which he knew everyone in attendance would drink. He poisoned us with some sort of toxin that induces violent behavior so everyone would kill each other and-" Ifra went silent when she heard Donard's shush.

The three of them waited in silence. Behind them, Ifra could hear the sound of shuffling feet slowly moving towards the door. Before them, Donard looked at a body sitting against the wall ahead. The body wasn't moving so the dwarf inched forward reservedly. The others followed, Ifra holding Bimblewald by the shoulder as they moved. The doctor could still see the dwarf in the ambient light, but the further in they were, the darker the short, stout silhouette became.

Donard reached down and felt about the body. The throat was slit and the clothes sticky with blood. The dwarf felt around and grabbed what seemed to be a candlestick. "Either of you got any matches?"

Bimblewald reached a hand into his waistcoat and pulled out a small matchbox that had remarkably not fallen out. He handed it forward to Donard, and the dwarf struck it to light the candles. The other two saw the body now in the warm glow of the flame.

"I know this man." Ifra said.

"Who is he?" inquired the dwarf.

"He's the chamberlain. He oversees the management of the Baron's trade through Verdendale."

"That's quite unhelpful then. The cook said the Chamberlain had lost his key to the gates." Donard began rummaging around the Chamberlain's body. *Might not have that key*, he thought to himself, *but that doesn't mean he ain' have somethin' valuable.* He felt around for a bit until he pulled a small key from the man's coat. "What's this open then?" The dwarf asked.

"The Third Floor is restricted to guests." Ifra replied. "Perhaps that key opens doors up there?"

"What's on the third floor?" Inquired Bimblewald.

"The Private Quarters. Only accessible to the Balteshezzar family and whomever they may choose."

"Could the baroness be up there?" Asked the dwarf.

"Yes! And the Baroness would have a key to the gates." concluded Ifra, feeling a small sense of hope.

"Right, well how do we get up there then? We can't go back through there lest you want to contend with the living dead." Bimblewald added. Somewhat apropos, they all three heard the door begin to shudder. The walking corpse had come to the door, and was trying to get in.

They all searched the room for a way out. Up and down the rows of shelves lined with casks of wine they search desperately. There was nothing, or so they thought. Donard finally returned to the Chamberlain and noticed something. The man was sitting against a wall, and beside him stood a solitary wine cask elevated on a stand and flush against the stone wall behind. Donard felt the wall behind the body and eventually found cracks in the wall, straight cracks in the shape of a doorway. He banged against the stone and sure enough, the wall behind the chamberlain's body was hollow. "I've got a way out!" Donard called to the others, who hurried back to his side as the rattling from the cellar door became louder.

Donard looking quizzingly at the out-of-place wine cask. "What are you doing, Donard? Make yourself useful and draw that pistol!" Bimblewald cried over the sound of the violent shaking behind them.

Donard chuckled triumphantly and grabbed the cask by the tap, twisting it and stepping back. The sound of gears in mechanical motion sounded within the cask, then inside the walls themselves. Finally, a great rectangular portion of the wall hissed and came ajar from the rest of the stone brick face. "A secret fucking staircase!" Donard exclaimed. "What wickedness did our baron use this for, I wonder?"

"I haven't the faintest clue, but let us use it now before it's too late." Bimblewald began running up the stairs, Ifra following close behind. The dwarf took a moment and found a lever just inside the opening. He pulled it and the secret door shut behind them.

22.

At the top of the stairs, Donard pulled another lever and another large rectangular portal opened in the wall. The dwarf pushed and slid the wooden porting to the right, revealing that they'd returned to the Baron's Office. "Fuck me sideways!" the dwarf exclaimed in hushed frustration.

"Well, at least we didn't have to go through the foyer." Ifra said. "There's a servant's stairway outside and to the right. It would be the fastest way to the third floor."

Bimblewald looked around the wreckage of the office--the desk split in two by the cleric's boot, the round window shattered by their escape--and felt disconnected from time, as if their experiences in this room were days ago rather than just hours. Why were they trying to kill him? He'd done nothing to them. He didn't even want to be here. Why had he even come? He should have just stayed with his circus and listened to stories by the firelight with his Esmerelda. Instead he brought Patch and Valentino here to die and felt the sinking feeling that he was next. Yet, even if he didn't die in this estate, would he ever be the same? What might this wizard's magic do to his mind, what lingering effects might the trauma of this night have in store for him? Maybe... maybe it'd be better if he died here.

Images flashed in his mind of the cleric bursting through the door. Something was different in the memory though. For a moment it was like he was looking through the Cleric's eyes, and instead of seeing the three of them, he saw... "Hey," Donard's voice broke the memory, "take a look at this."

The dwarf was holding a book that looked to have flown from the desk. He flipped through the pages and read it to them. "Seems like a ledger of some sort."

"The chamberlain would have kept records of the trade going through the town." Ifra said matter-of-factly.

"Well sure, but what're these?" Most of the goods were marked as being transported by Richard and Sons Riverboats and Freight. The goods Donard pointed out were sent by an independent Riverboat, owned by a Mr. Festibar Steele. They were regularly spread out over the course of the year. Donard thought there was something familiar about these goods.

"It just seems like a random assortment of commodities. Jewelry, porcelain, alchemical ingredients..." Ifra observed.

"But look here," Bimblewald pointed to a number of other items, "these are strangely notated. They appear to be logs of some sort, marked as 'Intelligence.'"

Donard began to come to a sudden realization. These items in the ledger were records of his robberies. His employer was the High Baron! "What about this though?" Ifra broke Donard's epiphany. The doctor was pointing at several items transported by the independent ferryman. "They're ... names. They're people's names."

Donard's anxiety peaked. He'd never kidnapped anyone, but it would appear that the Baron *was*, and was selling them no less. *What part did I play in all this?* he wondered, horrified at the idea that he'd helped in an underground slave trade.

"All of the items transported by this riverboat were sent to someone named Eldrik in Saint Alasthine, the capital." Bimblewald pointed out.

"Except for this one," Ifra indicated an entry labeled *Package 1291*. The package had three components notated as *1291a, 1291b,* and *1291c.* It had been sent to one 'Lady Animus' in the barony of Traceland to the northeast Verdendale. "I wonder what that is, and who is this 'Lady Animus'?"

Donard had separated himself from the others as they continued questioning each other over the ledger's contents. He was a thief, and an honest one, or so he thought. He'd always thought his employers were just some gang looking for people in the area to do some dirty work, and maybe they were, but they weren't stealing *from* the 'big hats' as he'd always imagined. They were stealing *for* them, *he* was stealing for them.

But why? Why use him to steal? Surely the Baron could have just sent police to rob the public, spies to gather intelligence. Why use a complete unknown, a no-name blacksmith down by the docks. He looked back at the others and the ledger. The doctor had said the chamberlain kept records of all the trade through the city. Perhaps that's how they knew of him, knew that he'd been struggling for contracts. Perhaps that's how they knew they could use him.

That wouldn't explain why they'd ordered him to rob the estate tonight. If he was stealing for the Baron, then why would the Baron desire himself robbed? Unless... unless the Baron himself, or at least the chamberlain, were just a puppet of whatever group Donard had been contacted by. In that case maybe they wanted both of their puppets in the same place tonight, the place they knew they'd both die and the loose ends in Verdendale would be tied up.

Donard's thoughts went to the letter he'd received, the one meant to detail his target 'goods' for the evening. They hadn't specified anything. Their only directive was to rob what he could from the estate tonight, then meet them further up river. Donard cursed himself, he'd been tricked! Whoever these shadows were they'd made an utter fool of him!

The dark recesses of his heart cried for blood from these heartless cowards who'd drawn him to his fate in these gilded halls. Tonight was never going to be just another Honeysuckle Festival. It was always going to be the 'Honeysuckle Horror', and Donard had allowed himself to be corralled into it like cattle, as his own employer cleaned up shop by killing the whole damn town.

"I think it's time I told you two something." Donard started before the Ifra shushed him sharply.

"Something's in the hallway outside." the doctor whispered.

Donard turned his head and looked through the open doorway. In the junction of the corridors stood a body. It was utterly still, unnaturally so. Something told them that it was one of the corpses from the foyer, animated as its cold dead muscles were forced to move by some external force blaspheming the circle of life. It sniffed and searched about like a predator hunting prey.

The three companions hugged the walls on either side of the doorway. Donard and Ifra watched through the door, only able to see what the bleak grey ambience of moonlight revealed in the corridors. They saw three shapes passing in and out of the junction. They stood unnaturally straight and drug their feet as they meandered through the halls at an agonizingly slow and deliberate pace. They made no sound to one another as they stalked and again Bimblewald thought he saw a faint green glow in their eyes.

"Come on." Ifra said, "It just passed the corner on the right. If we're quick and quiet we'll make it."

They all moved in a line along the right-hand side of the corridor, careful to ensure their steps were light on the carpeted floors. The corpses stalked about, one down the hallway toward the foyer, the other two down the way opposite the companions. Bimblewald felt fear gripping his heart. He could barely see and in fact the darkness seemed to be crushing his lungs as he struggled to breath.

The shadows deepened around him, even as they grew closer to the ambient light from the foyer windows. Every step was heavy and demanding, as if his legs were begging him to stop under the paralyzing poison of fear. He felt his blood stop cold and his nerves drive to the absolute edge of sanity.

You cannot escape me, the Darkness chided him, *I am and always will be your master. The creatures of the night will hunt you ever after. Their hunger is insatiable, and their ferocity builds with each moment you evade them. Let them take you now and it will be swift, but continue and I swear you will suffer a slow and agonizing death before you come to me body and soul.*

Leave this place and you may live, but you will never live without me, for I have overtaken you. I have seen the secrets you've driven from consciousness for the hate of it. Just like this palace, your mind holds dark corners where murder and lust drive you to hysteria. Just as I have done to this palace, I will do to you. I will draw every shadow that you have repressed to the surface and no one will be safe from you again. Your family's blood will cover your hands, as it has always done.

Come to me and I can ease your spirit's suffering. Come to me and you will be free. You will be as all my servants are: lost, deathless in the unending bliss of a greater will. You will be free to consume, free to take as you wish, free from all the constraints this world has put upon you. You will be as all of your race once were: alphas, victors of the forest, hungry for the blood of the weak.

Come to me! It said, *Come to me! Come to me! Come to me! I am your god and you will come to me!*

Bimblewald's senses returned to him as he looked down the hallway. Donard and Ifra knelt beside a door beckoning him to hurry as he'd at some point stopped following them. Beyond them however, the image of a little girl stood at the end of the corridor. Bimblewald couldn't resist the flood of desperation that overtook his mind. "Esmerelda!" He cried as the ghost disappeared.

"Fuck!" He heard the dwarf say. Behind him, the bestial sounds of the ravenous undead turned towards them.

106

"Go! Go! Go!" Ifra called. Then, Bimblewald sensed his body being dragged toward the doorway to the servant's stairs.

The world became a dark tunnel as he was pulled up the stairwell. He saw three murderous corpses enter behind them, shuffling up the stairs with undeterred singularity of purpose. One grabbed him by the foot and suffered a swift kick in response. The corpses piled on top of one another, clawing and biting at them, dragging him back through the door. Then, a crack resounded in the tunnel and Bimblewald's ears rang in a head splitting high pitched scream.

Suddenly, the paralysis receded and his blood flowed again. He heard the dwarf shout for him to get his "ass up and move before I leave you for the ghouls, you son of a bitch!" He stood and ran until all three burst through the door at the top of the stairs. Octavius stumbled to the side as Ifra and Donard threw a heavy dresser from the other side of the third floor hallway up against the door.

Great thuds slammed against the closed portal for what seemed like a lifetime before ceasing. Then, all was silent as the three sat winded in the richest halls of the estate. Ifra wiped blood from fingernail scratches on her legs. Bimblewald looked up, and saw the looming, berserk face of the blacksmith standing in front of him.

23.

Donard jerked on Octavius' collar, shaking the old carnie violently. "What the hell is wrong with you?" The dwarf growled furiously.

Bimblewald couldn't answer with anything but a whimpering "I'm sorry."

"You're damn right, you are! A damn sorry mess of a man. You're supposed to be some sort of fucking adventurer right? Travellin' far and wide with your big tents, tamin' monsters and such? Sure, we all heard the stories of the 'Outlandish Octavius Bimblewald, circus extraordinaire!' but by all I've seen, *you're not him*. You're a wimperin' little welp, and I don't bank on dyin' to protect the likes of you. Now…"

"Enough!" the doctor interjected. "Enough, Donard. Can't you see that this behavior isn't of his own volition? He's suffering, possibly of the same affliction that struck everyone else here though in a very different expression, and the effects are getting worse."

"And why exactly should that make me give any more of a shit what happens to him, eh? You say it was the wine, yet you drank and for whatever reason, you're not trying to get us killed. *He* is, and if he's gonna keep up these antics, then we ought not have him with us, no way no how!" The dwarf dropped Bimblewald's collar, and the old man slumped to the floor weeping.

Ifra went to his side. Octavius was broken, his mind was slipping… but why? Then, the man's voice broke through the moans and tears, "Donard is right, doctor. I can't go on with you. Tonight I have been forced to relive something I had pressed beyond memory, something I did that I couldn't believe--I wouldn't believe. Yet the voices in the darkness spoke the truth my memories would deny. I…" the man sobbed pitifully. "… I am a danger. A danger without fail to those around me, even my family. You must leave me if you wish to escape this horror. I'll only cause you pain and suffering, as I did Patch, Valentino, and even my dear wife." At last, he sunk back into pathetic sobs.

The others looked at each other in surprise as he continued his confession. "I was drunk and I couldn't... I couldn't stand her. She was telling me to abandon the Circus. That it wasn't safe for our daughter. The travelling, the animals, the... freaks. She knew the Rosary Brotherhood would come for us eventually, to kill us for protecting those whom the clerics would see dead. We argued and she threatened to take Esmerelda from me. So, I ... hurt her, and such was my guilt that, once she had gone, I fled into the bottle so I couldn't remember it ever again.

Fate's irony affected me as the more I drank, the less I endeavored beyond the Heartlands to find and protect the objects of the Brotherhood's hate. Eventually, the adventuring stopped altogether and the Cirque became simple entertainment. The magic died and was replaced with the mundane. The practitioners of the arcane were replaced by those of illusion, and the ostracized, deformed, cripples and elderly became little more than slaves to me, no matter how well I sought to treat them.

My adventures *were* real Donard, but after I lost my beloved... I couldn't imagine a life so fraught with danger for my Esmerelda. So, I became a coward in a champion's trappings, with the breath like a brewery and a soul half-dead. Perhaps that is why I am lost so quickly to the calls of the darkness and the dead: because I am already so close to being one of their number, regardless of my beating heart." Bimblewald's face went cold and lost in thought.

The others were speechless for a moment before Donard said, "Hah! A bleedin' heart more like. I'm going to check the halls." As the smith walked away he could be heard grumbling "... carnival master... no lack of melodrama..."

Ifra stayed with Bimblewald. The doctor was a specialist in anatomy, surgery, and even had some light study in neurology, but this was no disease of the mind brought on by a disruption of the humors or an infection. This was... deeper, a trauma to the man's psyche so integral to his being that he'd been unable to imagine life beyond it, to devise an identity for himself beyond that of an abuser. Moreover, it would seem that the toll of this trauma was being exasperated by whatever toxin had been released into his system, and perhaps even by the dark forces lurking in the estate.

Yet, despite this, Bimblewald had not gone insane alongside the rest of the guests. Why? If he was so unhinged then why wouldn't he have lost himself to whatever ritual of death had consumed the minds of the others? Ifra pondered this and concluded that perhaps the trauma had not destroyed his former identity, but had rather wounded it or obstructed it from developing further. Perhaps the 'Outlandish Octavius Bimblewald' wanted something so deeply, deeper than even the trauma itself, and would not give up the will to have it again. "Your daughter, Mister Bimblewald. Was she in the estate tonight?" Ifra asked.

"No. No she wasn't."

"Then why did you call for her before? Why do you keep seeing her here? I thought you were looking for the baron's daughter."

"I was, I think, but something, some*one*, is vexing my mind. The baron's daughter and mine, they blur until it's as if I can't differentiate them, and then these... hallucinations just... I can't help it. I need to save her--them."

"Why must you save them?"

"Because if they die, they're just two more people I've abandoned in selfishness."

"You *will* see your daughter again, and perhaps with medical treatment, you don't have to be a danger to anyone anymore."

Octavius looked up through his bloodshot eyes. "I wish I could believe that, doctor. Yet, even if we should escape this horror, I could not see her for shame."

"You cannot give up on yourself, my friend. You cannot give up on her. It will be the end of you if you do. Stay with me. We are so close to escaping this place. Come," Ifra stood and offered Bimblewald a hand, "Let's find Donard and get the hell out of here."

Octavius hesitated a moment and cocked his head as if listening to something, then shook and took the doctor's hands. Ifra let the carnie take the lead and the two went down the corridor and found Donard unlocking a set of double doors in a hallway to the right.

"No undead here, yet." the dwarf said, "He goin' to be alright?" He asked the doctor.

"I believe so, but we must hurry. Whatever the toxin or curse, it weighs heavy on the man's wounded mind or such is my hypothesis at least."

"Right, well, no one was in the baron's bedchambers, nor the childrens' so I figured I'd check the library next."

The other two nodded, Bimblewald weakly, while the dwarf twisted the chamberlain's key in the hole and opened the two doors. Once inside, Ifra closed the doors behind them and began barricading it with whatever loose furniture she could find. Donard stepped forward warily and spied something moving behind a desk on the other side of the room. Then a shout broke the silence and the smith felt a thud in the back of his head, then splitting pain.

"Bah! what the fuck?" He shouted and the woman dropped a long metal reacher to the ground.

"You are not mad!" The woman spoke with a thick flowery accent.

"Thank heavens, it's the baroness!" Ifra said.

"Indeed, and you are the new physician my husband hired from abroad."

"I am Ifra bint Sabadi Al-Jintra, your grace."

"And who are these you've brought with you? Speak!"

"Uh, I am Octavius Bimblewald of the Cirque de Bimblewald, your grace." The carnie spoke shyly.

"Donard Jünghoeffer, your 'bitch-iness'!"

"How dare you?"

"How dare I?" Donard replied incredulously. "How dare you? Oh yes, we uncovered your little side deals, *baroness*! We know exactly what you and your bastard husband were up to, and I know exactly how you roped my ass into it. Quite frankly, I'm more than a little pissed off about the whole mess, so hows about you hand over that gate key you've got stashed away somewhere in that corset and I'll be on my fuckin' way to farthest mountain minin' town from here there is!" Donard held out his hand to her and furrowed his brow unapologetically.

The Baroness looked at the doctor desperately. "Would you someone talk to your employer with such a tone?"

"I was hired to do two things, grace: treat the needs of the ill and research medicine. Tonight I have been forced to kill the wounded and sick, I have been forced to abandon nearly all hope of understanding whatever poison drove your people into such barbarism short of the occult, which I have neither an interest nor a liberty to do, as you well know. So, your grace, I feel I have no reason to believe that you have upheld my employment contract nor to see any solidarity you may wish I had with you. The key, if you please."

"By all the Saints, it's treason!" The Baroness backed away from them and ran to the desk.

From behind, a young man arose and brandished a small antique parrying dagger toward them. "I won't let you hurt my mother, peasants!" He cried.

Donard growled in frustration. "I'm not gonna hurt her, welp," he stated, "but I *will* kill her if she keeps that key from us."

Bimblewald stepped forward to try to ease the situation, then he saw a young girl rise from behind the desk. "Esmerelda?" He gasped.

"Mister Bimblewald?" the girl asked in surprise. A smile started to cross her face before she saw Donard pull out his gun and point it at Bimblewald.

"You go shit-for-brains on us again and I'll put you down like a rabid dog, carnie." Donard stated.

"Octavius, remember what we talked about." Ifra said. "It's not Esmerelda, it's Leona Balteshezzar."

Bimblewald paused for a moment, looking between the doctor and the girl, then shook his head with apparently great effort. "You're right, doctor. Yes, L… Leona. It's Octavius Bimblewald from… from the foyer. Have you been hurt?"

Before she could answer, Donard turned the gun from Octavius to the baroness saying, "Good, now that we know he ain't crazy we can get back to business." Then, Thomas Balteshezzar cried and ran for Donard with the dagger. Without hesitation, the dwarf turned the gun on the boy, "Back off, pipsqueak, or you catch one too! I am not fuckin' around, right now. Give me that damn key!" Then from the right, another presence entered the room.

They all stopped and from a book shelf that had apparently opened from the wall just like in the office, the baron himself came shambling into the room. The three companions saw him for what he was, an undead animation. The baron's wife and children however had no knowledge of the man's death at the hands of the Rosary Brother. "Father! Help!" Thomas called. The baron cocked his head at the boy, then in a flash and darted forward like a mad ape, eyes glowing a ghoulish green.

The boy barely had time to scream before his father was on him, ripping his throat out and slamming his head into the ground. The ladies screamed as the Baron rushed at them next. "No!" Bimblewald roared as the baroness tried to put herself between her husband and the young Leona, but she wasn't fast enough. The girl's screams were muffled as the baron wrapped her face in the palm of his hand and threw her from the window behind the desk.

The baroness wailed in agony and ran to the window with only a fool's hope that she'd catch her daughter. The Baron took his wife by the waste and sank his teeth into her neck and breast.

"No!" Bimblewald shouted again, running to grab a poker out of the library fireplace. Before he could attack the creature, the baron looked at the three of them and dashed into the secret passage, dragging the gurgling baroness behind him.

24.

Without a moment's pause Donard rushed after the Baron, delving into the darkness beyond the bookshelves. Ifra stepped to follow, but noticed Bimblewald shakily approaching the window behind the desk. "Octavius?"

"She can't be... He..." Bimbelwald reached the window and looked down into the West Lawn, where below he saw the mangled body of young Leona Balteshezzar, but to the old carnie, all he saw was Esmerelda lying in a pool of her own blood. Bimblewald felt sick and stumbled backward covering his mouth.

The doctor rushed to his side and grabbed him by the shoulders. "Octavius, please! We must follow our friend. We *must* get the key and get out of this place."

"I can't." Bimblewald gasped between heaving moans. "I can't!"

"You can. Just breathe." Ifra squeezed Bimblewald and began taking deep breaths. Bimblewald joined her and felt his nerves calm. The doctor took him by his arm and pulled him from the window gently.

As they entered the darkness of the passage they looked down and for the first time since their first escape from the office window, they saw lit candles. Before them was a winding staircase descending deep into the hill beneath the estate, and at regular intervals were candles burning a ghostly green flame.

Ifra and Bimblewald saw the Baron rushing down the stairs, Donard close behind. As they followed, they felt an incredible sense of dread wash over them whenever they passed by one of the candles. It was as if looking into the flames was like looking into the grip of death itself, lost in the mystery of the beyond.

They averted their eyes from the lights and continued their descent until they reached a landing on their right. Donard had stopped following the Baron and waited for them to catch up. "Why did you stop?" Ifra asked.

"There's someone in the room over there." He pointed toward a door inside a square chamber cut in the stone. "I could be wrong but... I think it might be the native I met." The dwarf went to the door and started picking the padlock.

"Why would they be down here?" Ifra asked. "Wherever here is."

"I don't know, but if there's gonna be a fight over that key down there, she'd be useful. She knew how to fight, from what I saw. Oh! For fuck's sake..." The old smith put away his thieving tools and drew the pistol, loading it, loading it with the last six rounds left. Enough, he hoped, to get out of this place if they were quick enough. "Back up." He grunted toward the others and covered his eyes as he shot the padlock off of the door.

"Careful, we don't know what else is in there." Bimblewald cautioned.

"There ain't nothin' else here but the native from what I saw." Donard dismissed Bimblewald and pushed open the door. Inside was a round chamber, and in the center was indeed the native woman, stripped and tied to a chair. "Give her a look, doctor." Donard said, prompting Ifra to move to the woman's side.

She was beaten badly. Bruises and cuts were strewn across her exposed skin. Her eyes were held open by a series of hooks and wires tied to the back of her head, or at least they had been. One eye had ripped through the hooks and was closed with a gashed flap hanging sideways revealing a small amount of the eyeball beneath. Finally, underneath her nails were twisted screws.

The open eye flicked to Ifra. "Who are you?"

"I am the doctor of the estate. I am here with Donard, the dwarf. He says you've met." Ifra explained.

"The dwarf? He was supposed to get the key and leave. Get everyone else out. Why are you still-"

"What do ya think I'm doin' down here, miss? Satisfyin' my curiosity?" Donard interrupted. "The only key we could find was just dragged to the bottom of this hole around the neck of the Baroness, by her undead husband no less."

"Undead? Then I've failed."

"Failed what?" Bimblewald asked.

Ifra brought a small tool over from a table nearby, one that had likely been used to the torturous effect of the poor woman, and pulled the dose of Dratha Root from her bag and approached the prisoner. "We're going to need to remove these screws before we unbind you, my lady. Please take this, it will raise your pain threshold."

The woman nodded her head with a terrified expression, ingested the drug, and bit down on the tool. Then, Ifra carefully removed the hooks from her eyelids and began removing the screws from beneath her nails. Bimbelwald winced and looked away as the native cried and nearly gnashed the tool to splinters. Tears rolled down her cheeks unevenly as some rolled through the rip in her eyelid.

The drug took effect quickly and the elf looked about with a flat stare as Ifra removed the last screw. Donard unbuckled the straps at the elf's feet and hands, saying "Great, now that she's drugged out of her wits, she'll be of great use to us."

"Her pain threshold was raised, not eliminated. The root's effects prevented her from going into shock, and likely prevented her death. She'll be quite normal in a moment as the pain recedes."

"What was her purpose here anyways?" Bimblewald asked.

"She said somethin' about a criminal of some sort that she'd tracked from the Sovereign Isles to here. She said he was plannin' on doin' something terrible."

"I suppose then that the necromancer behind all this was her fugitive."

"That seems most likely." Ifra agreed.

"This… is true. I was sent by my tribe's chief to hunt the greatest threat to our people that the colonizers have yet posed, a man who'd turned against his people and allied himself with the wicked Prime Minister, Lord Brigmond. I tracked him to Saint Alasthine, where I discovered he'd become the new leader of the Rosary Brotherhood. He was using Necromancy to turn the paladins into his undead slaves. I was to put an end to him, but there was never an opening, until now."

"You're saying that the Grand Lion is a Native?" Ifra asked.

"I thought the clerics hated the natives?" Donard put in.

"Also, why would the Rosary Brothers let a sorcerer into their ranks? They abhor magic." Added Bimblewald

"Yes, he is from among the tribes of the Sovereign Islands. He uses a combination of magic, cosmetics, and money to keep his heritage secret. As for the cleric's disdain for sorcery, it is a ruse. They do not kill magic-users. They only kill the ones they do not 'recruit'."

"Recruit for what?" Ifra inquired.

"An army." The woman said grimly, expression slowly returning to her eyes. "An army in the shadows, preparing for a war that will bring all mortal life under the heel of Lord Brigmond. The Prime Minister's ambitions extend beyond the First People's lands. Alasthia is just the beginning of his intended conquests and the 'Grand Lion,' Aldrich has lost himself in a vain pursuit of power. He has become a lich, nothing less than a deity among the dead, a god to all mortal souls. He is beyond comprehension now, a servant of greed and mercilessness.

Through him, Brigmond intends to commit genocide on what remains of the First Peoples, and all will become death and decay. The light of our lives will be blotted out, and the winds of the world will. From the darkness beyond the heavens will come horrors unspeakable as all becomes anguish and murder. The wise will hang themselves, and mad will relish at the taste of their own flesh. Women with children will drink poison, and warriors will drop their arms to flee for their graves only to find no refuge, for death will hold no solace to mortals whose minds can be dominated in death or life by the will of wicked spirits."

"I think that drug may have been more potent than you thought, doctor." Donard interrupted with an indignant roll of the eyes.

"You feel it too, don't you?" The woman, ignoring Donard's comment, said looking at Ifra and Bimblewald. "You drank of the cursed wine, yes? Tell me you don't feel Aldrich's tendrils weaving their way into your mind, manipulating your innermost thoughts, dominating your senses!"

Ifra hadn't felt such things, or at least she didn't think so, but Bimblewald identified strongly with the woman's words. "Neither of you can leave this place unchanged." She continued. "Lich sickness is debilitating and in-curable."

"Everything has a cure." Ifra said. "We'll find it. But first, we must get out of here."

"Right, let's get about that." Donard concurred. "Can you walk, woman?"

"I can." She said rising from the chair and wincing a bit. She walked over to the table covered in her torturers' toys, then behind to a chest. Opening it she drew out an obsidian knife. "Come," she said strongly, "let's go get that key. Someone must get the word out that Lord Brigmond is behind all this." They exited the door behind her and began their descent of the stairwell, the ghostly green ambience of the candles drawing from within them nothing less than desperation to escape this place and return to the land of the living.

25.

Down into depths, the four companions delved, the stairs seeming to go on in an endless dizzying spiral down into darkness. Less and less, the ambient moonlight from the library broke the darkness until only the spectral candlelight gave sight to their eyes. The flames taunted their senses as if they had wills of their own, showing them only as much of the stair in front of them as it wished. When Bimblewald looked into the fire for a moment too long, he thought he saw eyes in the flame, as if the blaze itself was watching their descent mockingly.

He felt weak and small compared to the primordial shadow of the depths that prevailed between the evenly dispersed lights. "What is your name, miss?" He asked the native woman to break their silence.

"You may call me Jetha." She responded.

"May I ask you something, Jetha?"

"That will depend on what you ask."

"The Grand Lion, Aldrich. What power does this man have exactly?"

"There are no simple terms for what Aldrich has become. I cannot describe to you the madness of lichdom, the cosmic blasphemy of attaining immortality in such a fashion. You cannot even conceive it when I tell you that your soul, your mortal connection to the preternatural state of being, the most incomprehensible aspect of your existence, is a plaything in the hands of our wicked assailant."

"Is it magic then, true sorcery, that caused all this?"

"It is, and of the most wicked variety. Aldrich has been born again by malicious spirits from the shadows beyond the stars. Believe it if you will but Aldrich has an army now. Above us, an entire city has been converted to his cause, their lives snuffed out by his poison and their bodies usurped by evil spirits called by his incantations.

The three of us will join that army if we do not escape soon." Again, the native indicated Ifra and Bimblewald.

"You said we would catch something called 'Lich Sickness.' What is this illness?" Inquired the doctor.

"As I said before, Lich Sickness is debilitating, in-curable, and that you would not leave this place unchanged. The three of us have already been affected by this plague. It is however a testimony to your resilience that you've lasted so long without becoming enslaved. It requires a strong will, a sense of self, to resist a Lich's consuming presence. The two of you are to be commended for that at least."

Bimblewald thought about this. Ifra hadn't shown any of the symptoms he'd had, and Jetha seemed quite uninhibited, injuries notwithstanding. If a strong sense of self was the key to resisting, he didn't quite know what that meant for him. His stomach sank at the thought of becoming like the beasts upstairs, the only thing giving him strength being his overwhelming desire to see Esmerelda again. He had to get back to Esmerelda, at any cost. He was a father, no matter what else.

But are you? He thought, or rather, he *thought* that he thought. It might have been more accurate to say something thought for him. The image of his wife leaving his life struck his mind again and again, each time with more detail than the last. How he'd brutalized her at the thought of losing his daughter from him... over nothing! Over politics, over business, over everything *but* their love for her!

How could she? He couldn't have let her. He'd never have let her take Esmerelda from him, nor his circus. He was a carnie! A master of the crowds, an entertainer of the masses, a lieutenant of troubadours! He'd never give up his circus and he'd never give up his daughter.

At that moment, at these thoughts, the memory came of the nobleman who'd attacked him at the very beginning of the insanity. A familiarity grew between Octavius and the murderous gentleman, a knowing deep in Bimblewald's heart as to why that man needed to kill him. *The duel was all he'd been,* Octavius realized, *his honor was all he'd had, and the Grand Lion took that away from him. Galvanized him till he had no choice but to either lose himself in the horrific realization that all was meaningless or prove the worth of his lifelong obsession.*

Bimblewald sensed this same sensation. Meaninglessness, worthlessness, inferiority, irrationality, violence--all of these and more were the story of his life, except for Esmerelda. He deserved to pay for his crimes but not like this, not in this darkness. Even if seeing his daughter one more time proved nothing of virtue or redemption, he'd pursue it anyway. It was meaningless, but he needed it anyway and this Lich would not have his soul before he'd seen his daughter again.

As if in response to his bolstered resolve, the image of Baron Balteshezzar throwing his daughter to her death flashed through his conscious mind. If what Jetha had said was true, that this sickness would only get worse, then he was doomed to give in to the madness sooner or later. What if his last moments with his daughter were spent rending her limb from limb? What if to see her again was to sign her death warrant in the end? If that was the case, maybe it would be better if he ended it here helping the others escape.

Then again, Ifra might find a cure. If he ended his own life in the tombs, he'd become a ghoul in the service of the Grand Lion and who knows what suffering his body would cause then. If he escaped, maybe he could hold out long enough for the doctor to find a means for both of them to survive.

Just as he'd finished his thoughts the nearby sounds of gnashing and crunching emanated up from the darkness below. A few more steps and the four of them beheld the

Baron consuming his wife at the bottom of the chamber. At the other end of the chamber was an iron door from which ghostly light escaped through the cracks alongside whispers of untold obscenities that defiled the very air they breathed.

The Baron looked up with hate-filled eyes and roared at them like a tiger. Jetha drew her blade and released her aching ribs to assume a fighting stance. Donard drew his pistol and cracked off a shot that punctured the Baron's half-naked form and sent him stumbling back. The native dashed forward, a flick of the wrist and the razor sharp blade had cut through the baron's left arm.

Enraged, the beast grabbed Jetha by the hair and yanked her back, causing her to drop her blade. Donard charged and smashed into the Baron with all his momentum. They all fell backward with the beast as Ifra charged forward and began trying to pry Jetha from the baron's grip.

Octavius stepped forward and grabbed the obsidian blade from the ground. He looked at the cannibalized body of the Baronness and felt a rush of adrenaline. Full of fury, the carnie ran toward the tangled mess of writhing bodies and cried, "Move!" He raised the blade in the air and brought it down on the Baron's head, burying it deep into the ghoul's skull. Bimblewald released the blade when he felt the body begin to convulse.

The others all stood as Bimblwald thought he saw some cold shape rise from the Baron and fly through the iron door. Donard took a deep breath and cocked the hammer on his pistol. Jetha pulled the blade from the Baron's corpse and walked to stand over the Baroness's body. She reached down and pulled a chain adorned with a small metal orb from the woman's neck.

"Is that it? Is that the key?" Donard asked.

"It is."

26.

"I think it's about time we get out of this place, then." Ifra said to the quick ascension of the others. Silusia handed the key to Donard, and then the darkness of the chamber was suddenly expelled by a flash of sickening green luminescence.

Bimblewald looked into the light emanating from the now open metal door. Inside the undercroft of the estate, he beheld the true visage of Aldrich the Grand Lion. Octavius felt his mind crumble beneath the weight of the sight, which cannot be described with words for the horror. His thoughts devolved into a desperate and futile attempt to rationalize the magnanimous wicked blasphemy of light and life within the dungeon portal. Nothing in all reality seemed congruent with the Lich's Phylactery that hungrily consumed his every thought.

Each moment seemed like a dream as he watched Ifra devolve into a state of primal panic. The doctor had fallen to the ground hissing and moaning as if in some sort of hysteric seizure. Donard was pulling his hair out at the roots and screaming obscenities.

Jetha drew her blade, shaking off the Lich's effects, and charged into the undercroft, only to be intercepted by a huge zweihander of a Rosary Brother emerging from the epicenter of the light. She dodged the blade's swipe nimbly and returned with wild stabs that seemed to effectively kill the cleric. Her victory, however, was to no avail to no avail as another cleric's hands closed around her face, prying her mouth open with such force that her jaw ripped from her head and her crown flew back to Bimblewald's feet, eyes agape in terror and failure.

Then, out of the dreams a thick hand grasped the old carnie's coat and jerked him toward the stairs. Bimblewald saw Donard ahead of him with the doctor dragging along in his other hand. Octavius fell into his instinctual need to flee, grabbing Ifra and lifting her up onto his shoulders. Together, he and Donard hurried up the stairs with abandon.

Up the stairwell they ran, the deep thuds of the clerics' boots chasing them every step of the way. Finally, they burst into the library. Bimblewald set Ifra on her feet, his lungs strained for breath and his legs begging for respite. Donard began throwing the barricades the doctor had set earlier out of the way of the library door.

"Doctor?" Bimblewald asked. The doctor simply moaned in a fit of lethargy. "Doctor, we need to go now!"

Realization filled Ifra's eyes as she heard the sounds of the boots ascending the last few stairs. She rose and saw Donard open the door, then without a word dashed through toward the southern stairwell. The others followed her down to the second floor where the undead had filled the corridors.

Donard and Bimblewald rushed the few corpses between them and the juncture of hallways. Ifra tried to follow but was grabbed by one of the necrotic fiends and thrown to the ground. They struggled, both in a fit of total barbarism. Teeth ripped at arms as fists flew both ways until at last Ifra stood over a torn and mangled mess of a body that even in this state still reached for her, desperate to end her life.

Half a dozen more of the undead rushed toward her. The doctor grabbed at door knobs, all locked. She threw her shoulder into one of the doors with all her might, breaking it from its latch and swinging it open. A window on the right hand side of the room offered Ifra an escape. She tried to close the door behind her, but the zombified apes had already reached the door and threw her back with the force of their entry.

She dashed to the window, threw it open and began climbing down with all the speed and nimbleness of humanity's tree dwelling ancestors. The monsters reached the window and one grabbed her by the scruff of the neck, lifting her screaming back toward the room. They clawed and gnashed at her, blood beginning to gush from beneath her flesh.

Then, a crack of lightning and she was plummeting toward the ground followed by a few of the Grand Lion's servants throwing themselves after the doctor in wicked abandon. Ifra landed on her feet, distributing the shock with a tuck-and-roll, and looked to see Donard with a smoking pistol in his hands and Bimblewald at his side.

Ifra met with them and they sprinted toward the gate of the palatial gates. They passed the statues and hedges until they looked upon the southern yard and all hope was dashed. Before them was a horde of the mad and zombified, the entire city turned to the will of the Grand Lion.

Bimblewald looked and saw the entrance to the hedge maze and had the spark of an idea. A final, foolish attempt at denying that blasphemous lich the right to his corpse. "Follow me, fellows! Into the maze!"

"You've lost it! We can't go in there!" Donard shouted.

"Please trust me! Hurry, they're coming!"

Donard looked back and saw the entire horde rushing toward them in a cursed frenzy. With no other option, he and Ifra followed the carnival master into the shrubbery..

Ifra led them through the maze, her memory and muscles working in perfect adrenaline-driven synchronicity. When they were far enough away from their pursuers, Bimblewald stopped. The carnie then pulled a dozen rolls of firecrackers out of his coat pocket and set them in the hedge wall. "Ifra! Give me your scalpel." The doctor gave the small steel object to Bimblewald, who then picked up a rock and a dry stick. He struck the scalpel against the stone once or twice before the stick caught fire.

Finally he used the stick to light a number of the firecrackers then yelled, "Run!"

The three of them ran as fast as possible before they heard jovial explosions behind them, catching the hedge wall on fire along with a large portion of the horde that had caught up to them. The three of them climbed over the southernmost hedge wall and sprinted toward the gate, the maze blazing behind them.

They ran through the eastern yard, past the three great fountains and finally reached the gate. Donard shoved the small iron ball into the demi-spherical indentation. The orb hovered within the fixture of its own accord and then the latch opened. The gate swung free and the companions rushed beyond estate grounds just before the horde of corpses crashed upon them. They sprinted with abandon down the hill and out of the city before they turned around and realized they weren't being chased.

Instead, behind them they saw the entire estate engulfed in green flames that seemed to be spreading throughout the city. Bimblewald wheeled around and saw the tents of the circus. "Come on!"

Donard and Ifra followed the old man toward the tents until they stood just outside the carnival grounds. Bimblewald could be heard within, calling out names, especially 'Esmerelda.' No one answered. Finally, they saw him walking toward them before falling to his knees weeping.

"What is it?" Ifra asked.

"They're gone!" Bimblewald said. "They must have left when they heard the commotion coming from the estate."

"Where would they have gone?" Donard asked.

Bimblewald thought for a moment, steadying his tears. "East." He said when he was calmed enough. "They'd have gone East toward Saint Alasthine."

"Well, that's as good a direction as any to get away from this place." Donard picked up Bimblewald and dusted him off.

"Indeed." Octavius said, wiping his tears away. The three of them turned east and strode away from the ruins of Verdendale and the Honeysuckle Festival. Ifra and Bimblewald looked back one last time, and both felt the same sensation as they watched the city burning with ghostly fire. They felt the same fear and sense of insignificance as they'd felt when they beheld the Lich's Phylactery, and in the back of their minds they knew they were cursed with knowledge that no mortal should ever have known.

All heard the same ominous warning flood their thoughts: *You are mine. Whether tonight or a thousand nights hence, I will have your soul and when I do, you'll join the march of the damned. You'll feast upon the flesh of those you love and drink the blood of your kin. You'll be as I am, and you'll rejoice in it.* Neither ever discussed this, but from that night forth there was always an unspoken kinship between the three of them. Moments of lapsing sanity were met with a mutual understanding that one day, they'd all go mad or else die before the sickness overtook them.

Epilogue

Fifteen years later in a small mining settlement far to the west of Verdendale, Donard heard the bell to his shop ring. The cold mountain air whistled through the door alongside a gust of snow and a well-dressed man with a wide brimmed hat, one side upfolded and bound to the cap with a strip of leather like a musketeer.

The dwarf stood at the counter and watched the man meander around the shop wordlessly. After a moment, Donard's nerves ached. He hated the way these city folk took their time with life rather than getting to business. "Can I help you, sir?"

The man turned to face the smith, eyes hidden by the brim of his hat, but well-groomed mustaches and a single patch of hair beneath the lower lip signified that this was no average city man. Style like his was more common among the provincial nobility. Donard reached for a gun he had beneath the counter. "I said can I help you with anything, boy? If not, I'll have to ask ya to leave."

"Yes, I think you *can* help me with something." The man's voice was as smooth and proper as his mustaches' curled. "I'm in the market for a gun. Somethin' fit for huntin'."

"Sure, alright, well I've got a pretty wide selection of guns. What kind of game are you trackin'?"

"I'd like this gun custom-made, if you please. I have the designs with me. As for my quirry, well, let's just say this gun needs to be able to shoot the spirit out of a man." The city-slicker slid a leather case over the counter to Donard.

The smith pulled out the designs for the weapon. "Damn, son, this ain't a simple order. It'll take me at least a month to cast the individual parts and assemble 'em."

"Take all the time you need. It must be among your finest work, so I'm prepared to pay for the extra time it'll take."

"You some sort of bounty hunter, boy?"

"Some sort."

"Where from?"

"Nowhere anymore."

"Where's your money comin' from then?"

"Inheritance."

"Oh aye? Lost your family, have you?"

"Actually I was hoping you'd know something about that."

Donard looked confused. "Who *are* you?"

The man took off his cap to reveal dark hair and blue eyes. "My name is Marcus Balteshezzar, and I was hoping you'd tell me about how my family was murdered."

Donard felt chills roll down his spine at the memory of the horrors at Verdendale. He released his tight grip on the pistol under the counter, it's familiar grip stoking the trauma further, and stroked his beard to calm his nerves. "Yeah?" He said after a moment's thought, "Well, I uh... I reckon I can do that. Let's go to the bar and grab a pint or two. I'll tell you the whole story."

First Edition, September 2021
Published by coalescence publishing, LLC
authors@coalescencepublishing.com

Wyatt M. Southerland
author.wmsoutherland@gmail.com

Made in the USA
Middletown, DE
04 May 2022

65242242R10080